## "I know about Jeremy—our son."

Mark had learned about Jeremy's existence only a few months ago.

"I'm sorry," Hannah said softly.

"Don't be. I'm glad to be a father. Very glad. I'm anxious to meet Jeremy."

He didn't want to pressure Hannah, but he could hardly wait to see the boy.

"He's a good boy. He'll want to know you, but I have a lot to talk to him about before I do anything to unsettle him."

"Of course." He didn't want to cause his son any distress. Then a suspicion came to him. "Does Jeremy even know about me?"

"He's never asked. I read a book by this doctor who recommended waiting until a child asks about a missing parent—especially if…"

"You thought I was going to die."

Hannah flushed guiltily. "I prayed you wouldn't."

"And I didn't," Mark said, clipping the words. Everyone else had thought that he was going to die; he didn't know why Hannah should have believed otherwise. It still felt like a betrayal, though.

**Janet Tronstad** grew up on her family's farm in central Montana and now lives in Turlock, California, where she is always at work on her next book. She has written more than thirty books, many of them set in the fictitious town of Dry Creek, Montana, where the men spend the winters gathered around the potbellied stove in the hardware store and the women make jelly in the fall.

## Books by Janet Tronstad

### Love Inspired

#### *Dry Creek*

Visit the Author Profile page at Harlequin.com for more titles.

# Dry Creek Daddy

## Janet Tronstad

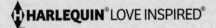
**HARLEQUIN**®LOVE INSPIRED®

Recycling programs
for this product may
not exist in your area.

LOVE INSPIRED BOOKS

ISBN-13: 978-1-335-50973-4

Dry Creek Daddy

Copyright © 2018 by Janet Tronstad

www.Harlequin.com

**Printed in U.S.A.**

Confess your faults one to another,
and pray one for another, that ye may be healed.
The effectual fervent prayer of a righteous man
availeth much.
—*James* 5:16

This book is dedicated with gratitude to those who make possible the many libraries in the places where I have lived—the latest being the women who staff the small volunteer library at the Covenant Retirement Village in Turlock, California. Their work brightens my days. Thanks to Jan A., Marge P. and Alice M.

# Chapter One

The sky was still dark when Mark Nelson pulled his pickup to a stop in front of the café, the only place in the small town of Dry Creek, Montana, that was usually open this early. The eatery's door was shut, but before he could switch his engine off, a woman slipped a delicate hand around the blind covering the café's large window and flipped the Closed sign to Open. His headlights were on and Mark saw a woman's profile and thought he recognized the hand. He wasn't fast enough to get a good look at the ring finger before the hand was withdrawn, but he told himself it had to be bare. He hadn't seen Hannah Stelling in four years—not since they'd been high school sweethearts—but surely someone would have told him if she had become engaged.

Mark shut off the engine and stepped out of his cab. The gravel under his boots crunched as he walked to the café and climbed the steps.

The one fact he didn't need anyone to tell him was that Hannah did not want to see him. He wasn't sure why she had moved back to Dry Creek and taken a job at the café, but a dozen Return to Sender letters told him that it wasn't because she missed him.

He paused briefly before turning the knob and opening the weathered door in front of him. The overhead light was bright inside the café and Mark involuntarily blinked. He heard the sound of a metal fork hitting the linoleum floor before his eyes adjusted and he saw Hannah staring at him across the empty room. She wore a red T-shirt and denim jeans. Her face was drawn, her auburn hair pulled back in a long ponytail.

"You." That was all she said, but her voice was stretched so tight it almost vibrated.

He recognized the look on her face. It was the same one she'd had over a decade ago when she appeared for the first time in the open door of his fourth-grade classroom. She'd been ten years old and had just been adopted by the Stellings. Her hair, a ragged copper cap, looked like she'd hacked at it with a kitchen knife, and maybe she had. No one was with her that day; Mr. Stelling had dropped her off and then left her to make her own way into the school. Hannah's stance in the doorway was defiant. Her jeans had a few worn places and her shoes were scuffed. The other kids were afraid to even smile at her. But looking into her eyes, Mark knew she was scared.

Since then, he must have lost the ability to read her eyes, because he could not tell how she was feeling now. Everything was silent as they stood there in the main room of the café. He heard the sounds of someone in the kitchen shoving pots around, and a radio started up on a station that must be the news. The half-dozen tables in front of him were covered with red-and-white-checked cloths, and everything looked ready for customers.

"Of course it's me," Mark finally said, not sure what else to do. Maybe Hannah just needed time to adjust. He surveyed every inch of her pixie face, searching for the subtle differences one would expect after a four-year absence. Her skin was ivory. Her bones delicate. Her hazel eyes so filled with shadows that they could have been black. She was twenty-one years old now, but looked the same as he remembered her at seventeen. He was only a few months older than her but it felt like he'd aged a dozen years since he'd seen her last.

He saw her lips move, but it took a few seconds for her question about whether he knew her to register with him.

"Of course, I *know* you." Mark was stunned she would think he could possibly forget her. He understood people were nervous around him because he'd been lying in a hospital bed in a coma for a little over four years. Everyone had been expecting him to die, but he'd held on and then he'd woken up. Some of his memory had been slow to return, but he'd always known Hannah. She had been his best friend ever since she had stood in that classroom door.

They both seemed like different people today, though. Back then, the two of them hid nothing from each other. Given the way she was staring impassively at him, he figured that had all changed.

"I'm completely recovered," Mark said and then paused. "Well, almost."

He had to admit that he didn't remember everything about the gun incident that had lodged a bullet in his brain and put him in the unconscious state, but he was fine. He certainly wasn't going to worry her about the gaps in his memory.

"Ninety-eight percent, at least," he added.

Hannah didn't seem convinced. She was studying him. "Then what's wrong? You had that look in your eyes when you came in—like you had something to say."

Mark winced. He had forgotten how well she could read him. "It's your father."

"You've seen him?" Hannah's face went blank for a moment. Then her cheeks turned pink with what looked like alarm. It was the most animated she'd been since Mark had stepped into the room. His heart sank. She could clearly be moved to concern, just not for him.

"I came from Miles City a few minutes ago and saw your father's pickup sitting beside the freeway," Mark said, telling himself to focus on the details. Hannah would want to know it all. "He had an accident about a mile out. I came along as the ambulance was loading him up." Mark had gone to the florist shop in Miles City and bought a long-stemmed rose for Hannah's first day on the job. "I was worried when I saw him."

"But that can't be right." Hannah shook her head as though her hearing was faulty.

"It was him," Mark said. She'd never questioned him before. Maybe she just didn't believe he was mentally able to tell her what had happened.

"I just can't believe it," Hannah said. "I only got back to Dry Creek last night, but he was out in the field behind the barn this morning when I left. I didn't have time to go out and talk to him then because I didn't want to be late for work and I had to take Jeremy to—" Hannah stopped abruptly.

She swallowed. Finally she was focused on Mark, but her stricken expression gave him no comfort. Her defenses were still there. He wanted her to be his sweetheart again, but she obviously did not want the same.

"I took Jeremy to Mrs. Hargrove's," she said, finishing her sentence and then gathering herself together before adding, "You remember the older woman who teaches Sunday school here?"

Mark watched a new, deeper blush climb up Hannah's neck and flood her cheeks with color. For the first time today, she looked vulnerable. Then she turned away from him.

"Of course I remember her," Mark said, trying to keep his voice even. "I grew up here, too." He paused. "And I know about Jeremy—our son."

He felt a hitch in his breath when he spoke of the boy. He had learned about Jeremy's existence only a few months ago. That's why he had been frantically writing Hannah those letters—the ones that had all come back to him unopened.

"I'm sorry," Hannah said softly and then looked away.

"Don't be." He reached out a hand to her. Her defenses were down and all he wanted to do was comfort her.

She took a step back from him. "I'm fine now."

"Of course you are." He withdrew his hand.

The biggest and best news he'd had when recovering from the coma had been that he and Hannah had a baby. Jeremy was four years old now. For months, Mark's sister and father had postponed telling him about the child since the doctors had said not to upset Mark. "I'm glad to be a father. Very glad. I'm anxious to meet Jeremy."

He didn't want to pressure Hannah, but he could hardly wait to see the boy.

She finally met his eyes.

"He's a good boy," Hannah said, her voice gentle. She smiled for the first time. "He'll want to know you, but I have a lot to talk to him about before I do anything to unsettle him."

"Of course." Mark bit back a retort. He didn't want to cause his son any distress. Hannah should know that already. But he supposed he could not just show up and expect everything to be smooth. Then a suspicion came to him. "Does Jeremy even know about me?"

"He's never asked." Hannah gave him an apologetic look. "I read a book by this doctor who recommended waiting until a child asks about a missing parent— especially if…"

It was silent for a moment and then Mark realized what had happened. "You thought I was going to die."

Hannah flushed guiltily. "I prayed you wouldn't."

"And I didn't," Mark said, clipping the words. He knew he was being unreasonable. Everyone else had thought that he was going to die; he didn't know why Hannah should have believed otherwise. It still felt like a betrayal, though.

Hannah was silent a moment and then she said, "I think you must be mistaken about my father. There are a lot of white pickups that look like his. About the only thing he said to me last night was that he was going to get the last of the wheat crop in today before the rain came. I know he was doing that this morning because he had on the same pair of overalls he's worn for years when harvesting. So, no," she said, looking at Mark with resolve. "He wouldn't have been going to Miles City."

Mark didn't know what Mr. Stelling had meant when he'd told Hannah he'd be getting in the last of the crop.

Mark passed the older man's fields almost daily. Mr. Stelling hadn't started yet and everyone else in Dry Creek had finished their harvesting.

It was the coma, Mark thought. People, and apparently Hannah was one of them, worried that it turned a person forgetful about the things that were happening in the present. But it didn't. He might not remember every little thing from before the coma, but he knew what he'd seen this morning.

"Maybe your dad needed to go for a new part for the combine," Mark replied calmly. He knew Hannah had mixed feelings about her adoptive father, but Mark always felt she secretly longed to be able to turn to the man like a daughter would, even if he was one of the most difficult men Mark knew. "He was wearing that old gray plaid shirt of his, along with those overalls. The shirt had a hole in the sleeve."

Hannah's eyes went wide.

"That's right," she whispered. "Mom bought that shirt for him before she died. He always wore it when he did the harvesting. And he had torn it the last year I was here. He never fixed it."

Hannah's auburn lashes were long and made her dark hazel eyes look striking. They were her most beautiful feature. But then, in high school he had declared her kneecaps to be works of art when he realized one day how pretty they were. It had made her giggle. Which had made him kiss her. Which had made her so breathless she started to hiccup. Which had made them both laugh. Mark wished they were back in that time.

"My father hasn't called," she interrupted his thoughts, bringing them back to the present. "He knows

I'm working at the café this morning. He'd call if he had trouble."

Mark didn't have time to answer before he heard the door open that led into the room from the kitchen. Lois Wagner, the other waitress who worked in the café, walked out to the area where he and Hannah stood.

"Here we go," Lois said in a pleasant voice as she held out a white butcher-style apron. She wore a red sleeveless blouse instead of a red T-shirt like Hannah did, but the middle-aged woman's jeans were just as well worn as Hannah's. Mark had gotten to know Lois in the past few weeks and he gave her a brief smile as she nodded to him. She was the one who had told him Hannah would be starting her new job today.

"The newest piece of our unofficial uniform," Lois said as she focused on Hannah again.

Hannah took the apron, but did not reach to put it on over her head. "My father just had a traffic accident." She spoke to Lois and then turned to Mark. "He wasn't hurt bad, was he?"

"I didn't see the other car, but it looked like a fender bender from what I could see," Mark answered. "We could contact the hospital. If he's unconscious, he can't call anyone."

"Oh," Hannah exclaimed, sounding even more worried as she laid the apron over a nearby chair.

"He probably only has a bruise or two," Mark said, wishing he hadn't said anything about the man being unconscious.

"If you want to go to the hospital, you should," Lois said as she put a hand on Hannah's shoulder. "I usually do the early shift by myself anyway, and Linda will be in at ten o'clock to help with the noon rush."

Linda Enger was the café owner. The staff at the café always said they couldn't ask for a sweeter boss.

Hannah turned to the other waitress, looking relieved. "You're sure it's all right? I don't want to leave you shorthanded. I need this job and it's only my first day."

"Don't worry," Lois said. "We might not get many people anyway since it looks like rain. It truly is okay. You can start tomorrow morning instead."

"I will check on him, then," Hannah said. "Just to be sure everything is okay."

"I'll drive you," Mark offered.

Hannah looked like she'd protest, but Lois spoke. "Let him, honey. I doubt you even know how to get to the hospital."

"No, I don't," Hannah said, sounding startled at the realization. "I know how to get almost everywhere in the county, but I never drove there. My father always did the driving when my mother was there."

Mark wasn't surprised that Hannah had never been in the hospital because of any need of her own. She'd had no issues except, of course, her pregnancy. She must have been in a hospital then. Mark's head started to hurt. The two of them needed to talk about the pregnancy. He hadn't known about the baby when they'd had their last big fight. He'd been in a coma when the baby was born, but he still felt guilty for not being there.

"I'll let you know how he is," Hannah said as she walked over to the counter and, reaching behind it, drew out a small black purse with a shoulder strap. Mark thought he remembered it as one she'd had in high school. He was going to ask her about that but then stopped himself.

From the bits and pieces she'd told him long ago, the foster homes and institutions where she'd lived before moving to Dry Creek had seen more than their share of petty thefts. She had not managed to keep much that was her own in those days. After she came to the Stellings, she guarded her possessions carefully. She believed she needed to fight to keep what she had.

She never mentioned it to him, but he saw that she treated the people in her life the same way. If she warmed to a person, she'd stand up for them against everyone else. People were not replaceable in her mind.

No wonder she was still talking to her father, Mark thought. If he didn't count Jeremy, Mr. Stelling was the only family she had. She wouldn't give him up unless she absolutely had to.

Mark opened the café door for Hannah and followed her down the steps.

He opened the door of his pickup and held her elbow so she could make the long step up to the floorboard. Long ago, his mother had taught him to be a country gentleman when escorting a girl anywhere in a truck. She said the young lady would appreciate it. Hannah didn't appear to think much of it, though. In fact, she scowled at him as though he should know better.

He was so dumbfounded that he just stood there a moment. She had never objected to his help. Not even when they'd been fishing and she'd gotten that long wood sliver in the palm of her hand and he had to pull it out with his teeth.

She couldn't have changed that much. Not unless something really bad had happened. It didn't take more than a second for him to realize he had been that bad thing. His coma had left her pregnant and alone.

He figured now wasn't a good time to apologize for letting her down, though. So he walked around the pickup, opened the door and settled himself behind the steering wheel.

In minutes, they were outside town and on their way to Miles City. He couldn't help but notice Hannah was looking down at the rose lying in the middle of the seat between them. She was frowning at that, too.

"Girlfriend?" she asked.

"Huh?" He was surprised, but managed to keep the pickup on the road. "No. It's for you. For your first day back home."

"Oh," she said. "I thought maybe—"

She stopped and looked out the window.

"What?"

"You were gone so long that I thought maybe you had a girlfriend now. That's all."

"I wasn't gone," Mark protested. "I was stuck in a coma."

"Of course, but—" Hannah started, but did not finish.

"I know I was still gone," Mark answered. He would agree to that.

Mark knew he should say something more, but he didn't want to give her a glib excuse. There was a time when he'd have been able to string together a convincing argument for his actions without even thinking about it. The bullet that hit his head had reduced his vocabulary to rubble, though. No words came to his mind and then it was too late.

"Nice day," he finally said.

"How can you say that?" she responded incredulously. "It's going to rain."

"I didn't mean the weather," Mark said. He wasn't

sure what he had meant, so he kept quiet. It was going to be a long drive into Miles City.

"This is it?" Hannah knew it was the hospital. That much was obvious. But she needed to say something. She'd been frozen in silence on the trip here, and now they were parked in the building's lot, just sitting there.

"They're planning to remodel the place," Mark said as he reached for his door handle.

Hannah turned to unlatch hers, too, and opened the door before Mark felt he had to come around and do it for her. She knew he was just trying to be nice to her, but she didn't want him to be polite. She remembered how, as a child, she'd felt like an outsider in Dry Creek, believing the town's friendliness was only for those who had been born there. But once Mark started coming around to take her fishing, she was content. She hadn't cared any longer if she didn't belong. One friend was more than she'd ever thought she'd have in life and she liked him.

But then Mark kissed her. Both sixteen at the time, they were standing in the far field checking to see if there were any chokecherries yet on the wild bushes that grew along the fence. The kiss had been an impulse on his part. She was sure of that. He seemed as shocked as she had been. But while he seemed to take it in stride, she felt like she'd fallen off a cliff. Something inside her shattered. After that, she dreamed of a future with him that she'd never given any thought to before that kiss. Suddenly he wasn't just her friend; he had become as important to her as the air she breathed. She'd never felt like that with anyone or anything before. No one had ever made her feel as safe.

And then—no sooner than she'd become adjusted to her new hopes—he was gone. Almost dead, everyone said. She hadn't allowed herself to get that close to any man since.

She'd been writing back and forth to Mrs. Hargrove over the years, and the good woman had encouraged her to trust someone, especially God, with her life. A few months ago, Hannah had decided to do that. But relying on God and trusting Mark were two different things. God did not go into a coma when she needed him most. No, she could not face that cliff again. Not with Jeremy being so very sick. She was all her baby had and she could not worry about anyone else, not even herself.

A long hallway ran along the edge of the building, and Hannah saw that the waiting room was crowded. A line had formed in front of the receptionist's counter.

She and Mark hurried over and joined the people standing there.

"It'll be okay," Mark murmured as they started to move forward slowly.

Hannah ignored his words. That was the way it started. A woman would believe some nonsense from the man in her life. And foolishness it was—no one could know if things were going to be okay or not. Mark should realize that. He couldn't guarantee anything.

Just then the couple in front of them finished their business and stepped out of line.

"I'm here about Elias Stelling," Hannah announced to a dark-haired woman behind the receptionist desk. "He was in a car accident out on the freeway about—" Hannah glanced up at Mark. "Would you say forty-five minutes ago?"

Mark nodded.

"Is either of you a relative?" The woman looked up from the paperwork on her desk.

"Well, I'm—" Hannah stumbled and paused.

She had run away from the Stelling place when her pregnancy started to become obvious. Her adoptive mother had died of cancer years before and her father still moved around the house like a disinterested stranger, glaring at Hannah if he noticed her at all. She had curled up in a protective ball when Mark went into his coma. She felt like she was in the emptiness with him, waiting to die. But there was the baby inside her, calling her to live.

After the first wave of grief passed, she knew she had to make some decisions. She was brittle and could break at any time. She refused to stay around someone who was supposed to care about her but didn't. Leaving the Stelling house was a stubborn decision based on hurt, but she knew it was right for her. She was better off in a home for unwed mothers, where she had no expectations of kindness as she did living with her adoptive father. Besides, she knew how to make it in an institution. No one could disappoint her. She never had gotten the hang of being part of a family.

She was taking too long to answer the clerk's question and the woman was looking at her with suspicion. Hannah straightened her shoulders. The hospital wasn't asking about the strength of her tie to the man she called Father. All they wanted was her legal status.

She nodded to emphasize her point. "I'm his daughter. His only family."

Neither one of them had anyone else. Strange as it was, that feeble truth had pulled her back to Dry Creek.

The woman still eyed her skeptically and asked for identification. Hannah pulled out her wallet and flipped it open. "Here's my driver's license."

The clerk seemed friendlier after she'd checked Hannah's name on the license. "We have to be careful who we talk to. The privacy laws, you know."

The woman looked down on her desk and pulled a clipboard from the pile in front of her. "The two of you can have a seat in the waiting room. Someone will call your name shortly and then escort you back to your father."

Hannah nodded. "Thank you."

Most of the seats in the waiting room were taken. Hannah noticed several mothers with toddlers and was thankful that Jeremy was not here. She was determined to keep him out of hospitals as much as possible. Planning to lead into telling him why, she'd asked if he might want to spend a night in a hospital sometime. The very thought seemed to terrify him. Since then, she hadn't come up with a good way to tell her son that he would most likely need to do just that because he was very sick.

"How's this?" Mark asked as he gestured to the two empty chairs in the corner.

Hannah nodded and they walked over to them. She'd have to tell everyone about Jeremy's leukemia diagnosis at some point, but she didn't want to do that until she had at least unpacked their clothes and gotten them settled.

She wondered how Mark could know who she was thinking about, but he seemed to because they had no sooner sat down in the chairs than he asked, "Which of these kids is closest to Jeremy's size?"

Mark seemed a little shy about asking.

She looked up and smiled. The first thing she'd noticed about him when he came into the café earlier was that he was wearing one of his rodeo champion belt buckles. The lights overhead made the buckle sparkle here and there where it hit the brass and silver parts. Mark prided himself on winning those prize buckles and had several. Today, though, he looked like the boy she'd met when they were both ten years old. He had a hank of hair that was unruly. It had always been that way. The rich brown strands curled slightly everywhere on his head, except behind his left ear. Tufts of hair just stuck out, defiant of any comb. Hannah had noticed last year that Jeremy had an identical spot developing on his head.

"The boy holding the orange ball is about Jeremy's size," she said quietly.

As Mark studied the child, she looked at him. Apart from the hair problem, he had a stubborn chin. It took the edge off his handsomeness. He had some fine lines on his face now that had not been there before. She wondered if they were from pain. Everyone she had talked to said he would never come out of that coma. When he started to get better, she had called the hospital. The doctors said they needed to be careful about his visitors and only his sister could see him. It had been the amazing story of the week on local news when he moved his finger for the first time, though. She'd wept happy tears for days. It wasn't until later that she realized everything would not just slip back into place. It could not.

"My sister says Jeremy loves horses," Mark said. "Maybe you can bring him over to our ranch and he can ride a pony in a few days."

She'd heard the Nelson horse ranch was prospering now that Mark, his sister, Allie, and his new brother-in-law, Clay West, were all working together. Mark's father was there, too, but he was semiretired.

"Jeremy would love that," Hannah said before she realized it could not happen. She didn't know exactly what his treatments would be, but she figured that, when they were over, Jeremy would be too frail to risk breaking any bones. Even if everything worked, the doctor said Jeremy might be in a wheelchair indefinitely. "It's probably best to wait a while, though."

Mark started to say something, but just then a door opened and a nurse called out, "Miss Stelling."

Hannah looked up. "This way please," the woman said. Hannah stood and Mark was right beside her.

The lights were bright and a series of doors led off the hallway. Muffled voices seemed to come from everywhere.

The woman motioned for them to stop beside a closed door, and Hannah glanced up to Mark. His face was pale. Those pain wrinkles seemed more pronounced. She reached out and took his hand. They had both lost loved ones in this hospital. His mother. Her adoptive mother. Mark squeezed her hand and didn't let it go. "We'll get him well again."

Hannah couldn't find her voice to answer, but she already knew she did not agree with his glib response. The coma had protected Mark from the struggles she'd had in the last years. She gently withdrew her hand from his. Mark couldn't help that coma, but she believed he'd already decided to move away before he got shot that night. He was going away to college. Her son didn't need to become attached to someone who would eventually leave him.

The woman stepped into the room and then came out.

"You can go in," she said. "The nurse inside will help you."

"Thank you," Hannah whispered.

Light green walls reflected the strong florescent lights. A grunt came from the elevated bed in the middle of the room.

"What took you so long?" a man's querulous voice accused her from where he lay. Blankets partially hid his face, but she knew him.

Hannah stopped in midstride. Her father had barely greeted her when she drove in last night, saying little beyond directing her to set herself up in the small house near the barn. That's where the farmhands had stayed when there were any. It was drafty and dusty. It hadn't been used in years. Her father had no reason to expect to see her standing here now.

"You can't talk to Hannah that way," Mark said before Hannah could answer. "You didn't call and tell her what happened. She didn't need to come to the hospital at all."

"It's okay," Hannah whispered. She was embarrassed at the gulf between her and her father. But she hadn't moved back under any illusion that he'd give her a warm welcome.

She'd come because she had no other home. And the part-time job in the café gave her time off so she could take Jeremy to his doctor's appointments. She'd still be able to work enough hours to buy groceries and, if necessary, pay rent. She reminded herself she needed to find out exactly what her father wanted in payment for use of that run-down house. She prayed it wouldn't be much; she didn't know what the copays would be on Jeremy's treatment yet—or even if their insurance would cover it at all. She'd find out on Wednesday when she took him to meet the physician who'd be treating him.

"No need to be touchy," her father said, glaring at Mark. "I—"

"We need to decide what to do," Hannah interrupted matter-of-factly as she stepped closer to her father's bed. She didn't have time in her life for this kind of drama. The nurse, on the other side of her father, was setting a glass of water on his table.

Hannah continued, "First off, you were in an accident."

"I know what happened," her father snapped. "My brain works just fine—" He looked over at Mark and glared. "Not like some I could mention."

"That remark is not necessary." Hannah was appalled at what he'd said. Her father never had approved of her spending time with Mark, but he'd usually avoided outright rudeness. "You should be grateful Mark drove me here."

She did not know what her father had against the Nelson family, but she wasn't going to let him make a scene. She stepped even closer to the hospital bed, thinking her father might lower his voice if she did so. The door was still open and she did not want the whole floor to hear him.

He just grimaced at her. "I don't need anyone hovering over me."

"Yes, you do," the nurse informed him briskly. "The doctor means it when he says you need to be watched for at least twenty-four hours. You've got a concussion and cracked ribs."

"I can't worry about any of that," he protested indignantly. "I have to get my wheat harvested. It's going to rain and I'll lose the whole crop if I don't get it in. Then how will I pay my taxes?"

"The doctor knows his medicine," the nurse said with even greater emphasis. "He won't release you if you're going to bounce around on farm equipment and do your head more harm."

"A rancher can't just ignore his crops," her father said. "He'll end up broke."

"The doctor thinks your health is more important than your crops."

"It's my livelihood," her father persisted.

"And this is your life," the nurse countered.

The room was silent for a minute while her father tried to stare down the nurse. He didn't succeed.

"I'll do the harvesting," Hannah finally said. "At least today and tomorrow."

She'd need to be free on Wednesday to take Jeremy to his initial consultation with the new doctor. But she could run the combine tomorrow. She'd helped her father with the farmwork the summer her mother had been so ill. He hadn't cared about the crops then. He'd sat in the back bedroom by her mother's side for days.

"You?" her father demanded incredulously. "You can't run that combine by yourself! Besides, you'd lose that job of yours at the café, and then what would you do? I can't be supporting you and that sick boy of yours all winter long."

The silence went even deeper. In the phone call she'd made last week, Hannah hadn't told her father about the leukemia; she had only said Jeremy was sick. Apparently that had been enough to put him off, though.

"I won't lose my job," Hannah said, praying it was true. "Maybe I can start in the fields before it's light in the morning—"

Mark interrupted, "Jeremy's sick?"

"I'll tell you about it later," Hannah said.

"Of course the boy's sick," her father muttered flatly. "What do you expect?"

It took Hannah a minute to realize what her father meant. "What are you saying? That it's my fault Jeremy's sick? Because I wasn't married?"

She knew how the old man thought. He didn't answer.

Hannah turned to Mark. "Let's go. He can stay here for all I care."

Her father's attitude reminded her of why she'd felt she needed to sneak away from his house. No one at the home for unwed mothers was even pretending to be part of her family. And that meant they didn't feel they had the right to condemn her, either.

She started walking to the door when she heard Mark speak.

"I'll run the combine," he announced quietly.

Hannah went back into the room.

"You?" her father sounded even more agitated as he stared at Mark. "Why, I can't let a Nelson—"

Hannah stared at the man who had been the only father she'd ever known. She wasn't the only one he disliked. He wouldn't ask for help from anyone. He'd locked eyes with Mark and was starting to sit up as though that would prove something.

"You need to get that wheat in a granary soon or you

won't have a crop at all," Mark said, his voice not rising. "You should have let me help you last week when I offered."

"You already said you'd help him?" Hannah squeaked, staring at Mark. She could not believe this.

He nodded. "And got cussed out for the effort."

Hannah glanced over to her father and saw him looking sheepish.

"You refused to let him help you?" she asked. "Why?"

Her father might not ask for assistance, but she hadn't expected he would turn it down.

"I don't need him to do anything." Then, looking belligerent, her father added, "And don't think I'm going to pay overtime for any twelve-hour days."

"It'll be more like sixteen-hour days since you let it go so late, and I'll not be charging you a penny, you old fool," Mark said. "You treat Hannah better and don't say a bad word about Jeremy and we'll consider ourselves even."

Hannah smiled slightly. Her father glowered at everyone, but he kept his mouth shut. He was apparently willing to accept help when it was free.

"You'll keep him quiet and resting?" the nurse asked Hannah. "For at least a full day?"

She nodded.

"I'll get the doctor, then," the nurse said. "It'll take a few minutes to get him ready to leave."

"My pickup is busted up, too," her father mumbled as the nurse left the room.

"I've got mine outside," Mark said. "Do we need to call a tow truck for yours?"

Hannah's father shook his head. "The repair shop has

it. I'll come back and get it next week. In the meantime, we need to take this back with us."

He pointed to a small cardboard box with a stock number on top of it that was lying at the foot of his bed. "For the combine."

Mark nodded. "That's the part you need?"

"Yes," the older man said. "I made the ambulance guys get it for me before I agreed to go with them."

Mark bent over and picked up the box.

"You were right, then," Hannah said to Mark as they exited the room. Together they walked back down the hall. The nurse was planning to bring Hannah's father to the left entrance when he was ready.

"I'm sorry he's so rude," Hannah said. "Hopefully he'll only need you for a day or two."

Mark looked over. "You're not responsible for your father."

"Maybe not," Hannah said. "But someone needs to apologize for him. He's gotten worse. I had no idea."

"He misses you," Mark said.

"I doubt that," Hannah muttered.

She reminded herself that she needed to stay in Dry Creek for only a few months. By then—*please, God*, she mouthed—Jeremy would be well again, at least if the doctor had an opening and could perform that new stem cell treatment she'd heard about. He'd already done it for others and had wonderful results.

"I'll pray with you, if you tell me what's troubling you," Mark said.

"Oh." Hannah hadn't realized he was listening that closely. Her words had been little more than two short whispered breaths. She didn't want to confess to her troubles, though. Not until she knew if she could trust him.

Finally Hannah nodded. "I didn't know you pray."

They had both been in Mrs. Hargrove's Sunday school class for years, so they knew their Bible stories. But by high school, neither one of them was taking God very seriously.

"You certainly didn't pray back then," she added.

Mark shrugged. "Things change."

She had no answer to that; it was obvious.

"We'll be back at your dad's place soon," Mark finally added.

"He won't sit quiet," Hannah warned. "You'll wonder why you ever agreed to help him."

"I'm not helping him," Mark said as he looked over at her. "I'm doing it for you and Jeremy."

Hannah felt the panic inside. "I don't need any charity."

Mark grunted. "Never said you did."

Hannah almost shook herself. Part of keeping her guard up was to do it so quietly that no one noticed. Mark would be watching her if he thought she was trying to avoid reasonable help.

"I can ask for assistance if I need it," she assured him.

"Of course." Mark smiled as he reached for the door.

Hannah let him open it and didn't say anything. This whole exchange was making her wonder if she could bring herself to ask for help in a crisis. She never would ask for herself, but she would have to ask for Jeremy if he was as sick as he might be. She'd know more after the upcoming doctor's appointment. For now, she had no choice but to accept Mark's help, even if it meant she put her heart at risk. She didn't know how she was going to cope with seeing him every day until her father's wheat was harvested.

# Chapter Two

Mark wished he hadn't bought the bags of feed that now filled the back seat of his pickup. He could barely smell the fading rose that had been lying on the seat of his pickup. The poor flower had no water tube. He felt a little foolish having it there now that Mr. Stelling was claiming that he needed to ride in the middle of the seat. It was difficult to be gallant and give a rose to a woman when the woman's father was seated between them. Mr. Stelling had his knee braced against the gear shift and Hannah was huddled in the opposite side of the cab looking like she was weighed down by the troubles of the whole world—not that she would admit it.

Mark figured he'd made a little progress with her, but it wasn't enough. It had been so easy to be her hero when they were younger. Now she wouldn't even talk to him.

"You'll need to get these shocks checked," Mr. Stelling complained as he pressed his knuckles down on the seat's padding. "Not very comfortable."

Mark put his vehicle into Reverse. He turned to give

Hannah a quick smile but saw she wasn't looking his way.

"Dad," Hannah protested, still looking out the windshield.

"Well, there's too much bouncing on the passenger side," her father said as he turned to face her. "A man needs to take good care of his pickup. Mark should know that."

Hannah turned to look at her father. "It doesn't matter. He's doing us a favor."

Mr. Stelling turned back to stare out the front window.

In all that time, Hannah hadn't spared Mark a glance.

"Your father just likes to keep me away from you," Mark said, hoping he'd get a chuckle from at least one of them.

Hannah didn't turn his way and Mr. Stelling didn't answer. The other man had a white bandage wrapped around his head, and he was sitting straight in the seat just like the nurse had asked him to.

"Not that I blame him for that," Mark added.

That didn't gain him any further response, so Mark kept silent as he made the turn from the parking lot to the main street leading to the freeway.

"I don't like hospitals," Mr. Stelling finally said. "They make me cranky."

Mark figured that was as close to an apology as he'd get from the older man.

"None of us like them," Mark agreed. They were crowded together in the cab, but at least now it didn't feel quite as awkward.

Within a few minutes, they were on the freeway and headed back to Dry Creek. There was little traffic. Large empty fields lined both sides of the freeway.

Mark refrained from mentioning that all those other ranchers had managed to get their wheat harvested. A herd of deer stood in the distance, grazing. The clouds on the horizon looked darker than they had been. Mark only hoped the rain would hold off long enough to get Mr. Stelling's harvest done.

"I shouldn't have made that remark about your head being damaged," Mr. Stelling offered when they'd driven a few miles. He was silent for a while and then asked, "Did it hurt much all those years you were out of it?"

"You mean during the coma?" Mark turned slightly. It was not surprising the older man would ask about that time. Everyone seemed curious. "No, it didn't hurt. At least, I don't think so. I don't remember much."

Mr. Stelling nodded. "My wife, she was in a coma a few days before she died."

"Ah." Mark understood now. He'd forgotten that fact. "Don't worry. She wasn't in any pain."

A few more miles passed. Mark wondered if he'd always be known as the man who'd been in a coma. People used to say he'd do great things in his life—that he'd be a hero. No one said that any longer. He even had some sensational grocery store newspaper call and offer him a "significant amount of money" to interview him for a story. The thought made him cringe. He didn't want to be known as the man who had been stuck in a coma for four years. A man needed some dignity.

Mark thought a moment. "I still don't remember everything about that night when I got shot."

Mark didn't want his life laid out to satisfy the curiosity of strangers, but he did want to tell Hannah how sorry he was about what happened back then, and this might be his only chance to do so.

"I'd called and asked you to come over and talk to me," Hannah said. Her voice was low, but she had turned so he could see her. He wasn't sure of her emotions from her eyes, but he thought he saw some hurt in their depths. He wanted to soothe it away.

"I remember that clearly," Mark said. "Your dad was at some church meeting, but I still parked my pickup out by the driveway into the ranch and you walked out to meet me. Some of your mother's flowers were blooming."

"The wild roses." Hannah smiled then. "You could smell them all along the fence. It was a moonlit night."

"They were a deep pink," Mark offered. "Beautiful."

Mr. Stelling grunted. "I would have grounded her for a month if I'd known she was seeing you behind my back. You never were any good for her."

"He was my friend," Hannah protested even though she didn't look over at him. "There was a bully at school and he always protected me."

"I still am your friend," Mark said. "I hope you know that even though there probably aren't any bullies now."

*Except for your father*, Mark added to himself silently. He figured Hannah wouldn't want him to say that, though. She didn't answer, and memories flooded Mark. He'd thought she had circles under her red-rimmed eyes that night because she was coming down with a cold. He hadn't realized until later that she had been scared and had likely been crying.

"I should have told you straight out that I was pregnant," Hannah said quietly. She did glance up at him then. "Instead, all I could do was pick a fight. I wanted to argue. I thought there would be time to tell you about the baby when you came back."

Mark shook his head. "It was my fault."

Her father grunted this time. "I'll say."

"Do you mind?" Mark asked the man. "We're trying to have a conversation here."

"You can't order people around," Mr. Stelling said. Then he crossed his arms over his stomach. "Who do you think you are, anyway?"

"I don't know any longer," Mark snapped back without thinking. On the day he and Hannah were trying to discuss, he'd known exactly who he was. He'd just been awarded a full scholarship to the college in Missoula. Everyone said he'd win at least two events in the local teen rodeo like he had for the past three years. He craved prizes like that. Somehow it was proof that he was somebody—a hero of sorts. He didn't think he'd see any more of those wins again in life. No one gave out brass-plated belt buckles to someone for learning to tie their shoes.

He glanced over at Hannah. He had defended her from everything once. Now he wasn't sure if he could protect her from anything.

"I'm sorry," he said. The least he could do was get on that combine and harvest her father's wheat. He didn't want her to have to do that. She looked tired to him.

"That night was my fault," Hannah said again, her voice firm. "I shouldn't have gone on like I did. You were excited about that scholarship and all I could see was that it was pulling you away from me."

"No," Mark protested. There was that flash of hurt in her eyes again. "I always saw that scholarship as being for us. For a chance to live a good life for us—you, me and—well, I wasn't thinking of children then, but it would have been all of us."

He'd never thought he'd be content to be a rancher. He had wanted to win all the prizes the world had. He pictured Hannah on his arm, looking proud. A big house. An important job. Lots of money. Truthfully, he didn't ever remember asking himself if that was the kind of life that Hannah would want, though.

"Well, if I hadn't been so upset, you wouldn't have gone off like you did," she insisted. "I knew that scholarship was important to you."

Mark shook his head. He wasn't willing to let himself off the hook that easily. "It wasn't about the scholarship. No one forced me to go out drinking with Clay. He didn't even want to go driving around. Besides, my mother had always told me never to start drinking. She knew my father had a terrible time with it and she worried I'd inherit that from him."

No one needed to say anything more. Mark had let alcohol overtake him that night. He became so confused he came up with the crazy idea of taking the hunting rifle from the rack in his pickup and going in to rob that gas station. He couldn't remember what he'd been thinking. But he still clearly saw the slice of time when he'd turned that gun on the male clerk inside the station and demanded money. Events had happened fast then. The clerk turned out to be an ex-marine and skilled enough in combat to disarm Mark. In the scuffle, the gun had discharged and the bullet slammed into Mark's head.

He sat there a minute, just driving as he watched the farmland go by. He was more content than he thought he'd be with his future on the family ranch. He turned toward Hannah. "Don't let Jeremy ever drink."

Until this moment, Mark hadn't realized that the Nelson curse of alcoholism could touch his precious son.

Hannah grinned and glanced at him over her father's head. "So far Jeremy hasn't asked for anything stronger than grape juice. That's his favorite. He tends to spill so he takes it in a sippy cup, but he's almost ready for a regular big boy cup."

Mark basked in the moment. This was the kind of conversation parents would have.

"The boy should be drinking milk, not juice," Mr. Stelling announced.

Mark saw Hannah bite back a response. He was glad they were making the turn off the gravel road. There was a lot of irritation in his pickup and only some of it belonged to him. Still, he was pleased to be escorting Hannah home.

Hannah felt her stomach muscles clench as the pickup turned into the drive leading to her father's house. The sky had grown lighter although it remained gray. The conversation had bumped along all the way back from Miles City, and she saw the scowl on her father's face deepen as he looked at his place. She figured he regretted the deal with Mark. But it was too late; Mark was already parking the pickup, and someone needed to run the combine.

"At least the rain is holding off," she said, hoping to ease the tension. Every rancher she knew liked to talk about the weather. The clouds were gray, but there had been no droplets on the windshield of the pickup.

Both men just grunted in response to her observation.

Mark opened the door on his side of the cab and she

did the same. She was relieved to step down onto the hard-packed ground. Maybe things would be friendlier now that they were home.

She startled herself by even thinking of this place as home. But she took a good look around. It had been twilight when she arrived at her father's ranch last night and dark when she left this morning. Now, seeing the place in full light, she noticed signs of neglect. Weeds had long ago overtaken her mother's old garden space. The buildings needed new paint. Every fall her father had hired a local man to grade the road from the house to the barn, but it hadn't been done in what looked like years.

She heard her father slide across the seat and step down from the pickup.

In spite of everything, she had some warm memories of living here. She hoped she would be able to do a few things to fix it up in the time she'd have.

"It's good to be home," she said softly.

Her father gave her a long look. Then he nodded curtly and started walking toward the house.

Hannah watched him make his way to the porch. She wondered if she could ever make her peace with this man. She'd heard sermons about forgiveness and figured her adoptive father was high on the list of people she needed to work on in that area.

She'd need God's grace to do anything like that, she thought to herself as she followed her father over to the house.

She walked up the steps behind the older man. Mark was right behind her.

Her father paused as he stood in front of the door to the house.

"There's no need for you to come in," he announced as he reached for the knob. He kept his back toward Hannah.

"Mark will need something to drink," she finally said, figuring the words must have been addressed to him. "Water, at least. Maybe iced tea. Operating that combine is dusty work."

She sensed Mark stopping next to her. She never had understood her father's grudge against the Nelson family. He'd had it before she'd been adopted and it seemed to be still active in his mind.

Her father turned then. His eyes narrowed as he looked at her directly. "I meant you, too. I can take it from here. I'll bring out a gallon of water if you both just take a seat on the steps."

His words caught her by surprise. She felt them slice through her like a knife. Mark moved closer.

Then, as her father started to push the door open, she realized what he was doing.

"Oh, no, you don't," Hannah protested as she reached out and touched his shoulder. He turned, but didn't meet her gaze. "I promised that nurse—the doctor, too—that I would keep an eye on you. You need to let me in the house or we are both sitting out here."

Her father hadn't invited her inside last night, either. Instead he came out on the porch to tell her that she and "that boy of yours" could stay in the small house by the barn.

"The doctor knows best," she added. "He said I was to check you out every fifteen minutes for the first few hours. I can't do that if I can't see you."

Hannah could tell her words were not convincing him.

"She's right. You have to cooperate," Mark said firmly.

Her father stood there, blocking their view of the inside of the house.

"My place is a mess," he finally mumbled as he went inside.

"That's not a problem." Hannah stepped into the doorway after him. She was glad to understand his hesitation. He was embarrassed. That could be fixed.

It was dark inside and it took a moment for Hannah to see everything.

"Oh." She looked around in dismay. The living room was not just cluttered; it had been dismantled. Ragged shades covered the windows and the curtains had been ripped off their rods.

"Mom and I made those drapes," Hannah exclaimed as she surveyed the empty rods. Her mother had carefully selected the deep-blue-and-gold floral brocade. She thought it made the house look happy. Hannah had run the sewing machine because her mother was so weak by then. Hannah looked over at her father. "She wanted to give you a place of comfort. An oasis."

Mark was standing behind her father and, when her father didn't look up at her, she raised her questioning eyes to him instead.

Mark shrugged. "Maybe he was too busy out in the fields to do much housework. It happens."

It didn't happen in this house, Hannah thought. Her father had been as meticulous about things as her mother had been.

For the first time since Hannah had come back, she was glad her father didn't want her and Jeremy to stay in this house. Her son needed sunshine and cheer if he was going to beat his illness. The house by the barn, even with the boarded-up window in the one bedroom, would be better than this.

Her father still wasn't meeting her eyes and Hannah felt sorry for him. "When we get the crops in, I might be able to sew up some new curtains for you."

Her father looked at her then before he shook his head.

"I'm fine," he said.

"How could—" Hannah started but then saw Mark give a slight shake of his head. She swallowed. "No matter. Let's see about getting a cup of tea made for you." She looked at her father. "I'm assuming you still like hot tea."

He nodded.

"No cream, extra sugar?" she asked. "English Breakfast?"

"Yes," he said. "I'll take it in the kitchen at the table."

Her father walked into the kitchen and closed the door.

Hannah looked over at Mark, wondering if he'd understood how hard it had been for her to find some common ground with her father. But Mark wasn't focused on her. Instead, he was staring at the wall behind the sofa.

She turned around.

"Oh," she gasped. What had gone on in this room after she left here four years ago? "My pictures are gone."

Her mother had set up the photo wall to display the annual school pictures that Hannah received. There'd been seven large photos displayed in gold metal frames. She had gapped teeth in the first when she was ten years old and smooth curls in the last photo when she was seventeen. Those photos made her feel she belonged here. The only things left on the wall now were the nails from which they'd hung.

"He had no right to do this," Mark said fiercely as he walked over to stand beside Hannah.

He knew what those pictures meant to her. Her mother had been so proud when she'd hung each one.

"I need to forgive him," Hannah said as she looked up at Mark. She blinked back her tears. "The Bible says so."

"But you're his daughter," Mark protested. "This is your home."

"Mrs. Hargrove told me he's stopped going to church," Hannah whispered. She'd not thought much about that revelation, assuming her father was just catching up on ranch work. Now she wondered.

"He has no one to blame but himself if he's lonely," Mark said as he took a step closer to her. She longed to lean into him like she would have when she was much younger. But she needed to stand strong herself these days and she might as well start now. She couldn't trust anyone to prop her up.

She shook her head. "My dad just misses Mom."

"We all do," Mark said and then paused. "Do you forgive everyone?"

"I try." Hannah remembered how Mark always seemed to know her heart. She looked up as he stood there. In a moment, the hard years rolled away and she felt a rush of emotions. Maybe it was nothing but nostalgia. She didn't know, but she had been in love with Mark a long time ago. She saw the same kind of emotion flit through his eyes before he turned thoughtful.

"Then why did you send back my letters?" he asked.

"What?" Hannah wondered if his mind was playing tricks on him. She'd never gotten any letters. Nor had she expected any since he was in a coma for so long. She'd taken Jeremy to visit him once in the hospital nursing home over a year ago, but Mark had not been conscious for that. Still, he was looking at her like he expected a response. "I—"

She was interrupted by the sound of a dish breaking in the kitchen.

"I better go," she said as she headed for the doorway. She heard Mark's footsteps following behind her. She wished he wasn't here to witness the problems with her father, but she had no choice. She only hoped he would leave before her whole world crashed down upon her.

## Chapter Three

Mark stood in the doorway, relieved to see the kitchen hadn't been as trashed as the living room. Yellow striped cotton curtains hung from rods on these windows. The beige countertop was worn, but empty of clutter. Mark was only beginning to understand the ripple effect of that night when he'd been injured. It hadn't been only his and Hannah's lives that had been thrown into chaos. His family had been hurt. Her father wounded. And Jeremy—what price had his son paid?

"You've kept the teakettle up nicely," Hannah said from where she stood at the sink. "It's polished." Her father nodded from his place by the refrigerator. She seemed determined to be cheerful as she turned the water on and began to fill the copper kettle. Mark remembered she had often done that when they were children. Most children would complain at least a little about their parents. Not Hannah. She just put on a positive face and pretended everything was all fine.

"I kept everything up," her father said as he walked over to the table. "That is, until—"

Mr. Stelling stood there mute before finally pulling out a chair.

Hannah's jaw tightened, but she was silent.

"Until what?" Mark demanded. He might not have much to offer Hannah any longer, but he could at least stand as her champion in this house. He didn't like that she felt the need to pretend to a satisfaction that couldn't possibly be there.

The older man winced as he sat down. "I thought she—" he nodded toward Hannah "—and the boy might want to come for Christmas. I decided I needed to paint the living room before I asked—"

Mark heard the kettle fall and hit the bottom of the sink. He looked over at Hannah. Her mask was crumbling. Wide-eyed, she was staring at her father in genuine gratitude. Her father might be cranky, but he was not her enemy.

"But you never even wrote to me," she said.

"I didn't have your address," her father mumbled. "I was going to get it from Mrs. Hargrove, but I thought I'd do the walls first. Then you called."

"But I don't care about the walls," Hannah said as she took a step toward her father. She was wiping her wet hands on her jeans as she went. "At least, not much."

Mark was struck by something else.

"You didn't have her address?" he asked her father.

The other man shook his head.

Mark had assumed Mr. Stelling would know where his daughter was. All of the letters Mark had written when he was recovering in the nursing home had been addressed to this house with the notation to forward them. No wonder they had been returned.

By the time Mark figured it all out, Hannah was

standing in her father's arms. Mark wasn't sure, but he thought there was a tear or two trailing down her cheeks.

*Lord, thank You.* Mark sent the prayer up as he watched the reunion between Hannah and her father. Mark would have given anything to be Hannah's protector again, but it was not necessary.

He had nothing useful to do for Hannah, he realized. When they had been children, he'd stopped that boy in their class from teasing her on the playground. Mark had been proud to do that. Even his mother had been pleased with him that day. Accomplishments like that had brought expressions of love from his mother. She beamed when Mark was on the honor roll. She cheered when he won races at the school track meet. She would have screamed encouragement at his rodeos if she'd lived that long. Being a hero in his mother's eyes had been the way Mark gained her love. He had always assumed that he would be able to lay similar accomplishments at the feet of Hannah and earn her love, too.

But his days of winning were over. He doubted he'd ever ace another competition. He'd had plenty of compliments in the nursing home, but in the real world, no one was likely to genuinely praise him because he'd remembered how to use a spoon.

"I was going to paint the walls eggshell white," Mr. Stelling said as Hannah stepped back. "Your mother always said that was a color that looked good in any light."

Hannah nodded. "Yes, she did say that."

Hannah's face wore the expression Mark had hoped to see when she looked at him. She was luminous with love. She just wasn't looking at him.

Mark glanced away toward the window. The sky was dark as gunmetal. It could start to rain at any moment.

"I'd best get that jug of water," Mark said as he turned toward the sink. He felt about as unnecessary at the moment as a doorstop in a room that had no exits.

"On the top cabinet," Mr. Stelling said as he pointed to a high shelf.

Mark nodded his thanks to the man as he reached for the gallon jug. That was the most civil comment he'd ever heard from Hannah's father.

"I've got the mechanical part you bought in Miles City out in the back of my pickup," Mark offered as he pulled the glass container down off the shelf. The replacement part for the combine had ridden there on the trip back from the hospital. "I should have the old one off and the new one on before long."

"I can help you with that," Mr. Stelling offered.

"The doctor said—" Hannah protested.

"I won't be doing anything much," her father replied. "The faster we get that new part on the combine, the quicker Mark can start harvesting the wheat."

Mark took the jug to the sink and turned the cold faucet on. He'd appreciate having some water when the day grew warmer. That is, if it didn't rain.

The water soothed him as he let it run. Crops and ranching had been deeper in his blood than he'd realized in high school. He wondered if he would have been content in the world of awards and money he'd dreamed of back then.

Hannah watched her father stand by as Mark filled the jar with water. The next step would be to wrap an old gunny sack around the glass and get the cloth wet.

The moisture on the sack would evaporate and keep the bottle's contents cool. It was an old rancher's trick that her mother had explained one hot day.

"I'll call Mrs. Hargrove," Hannah said to the men. "She might be able to drive Jeremy back here if I explain what happened today." She looked at Mark. "I hope you can eat with us. I'll have something ready at noon. I'm not sure what it will be, but—"

Mark beamed at her. "Make something Jeremy will like."

Hannah smiled. "Are you sure? That would be macaroni and cheese or peanut butter and jelly sandwiches."

"Fine with me," Mark said.

"The boy should have some vegetables," her father said gruffly. "He can't get over whatever ails him on macaroni and cheese."

Hannah felt the smile fade from her face. For a moment, she'd forgotten. "Food won't make any difference."

"How come?" Her father barked the words like he was a drill sergeant. "Vitamins and fresh air will cure most anything that's wrong with a young boy."

Hannah could see that her father was curious. It was Mark who worried her more, though. He stood there with a thoughtful look on his face.

Everyone was silent for a time.

"Is there anything I can do?" Mark finally asked. "Have you seen a doctor?"

Hannah nodded. "And I see another one on Wednesday. Then I will just need a little time to—"

She let her voice trail off. She wasn't exactly sure what she needed to do to prepare her son for his treatments. And she didn't want other people telling him things that might worry him. "I'll have more answers by then, at least."

"The boy can visit with me while I recover from my concussion," her father offered. "I hear from Mrs. Hargrove that he's quite the chatterbox."

"His name is Jeremy," Hannah said. "And he'd like that."

She hadn't told her son that he had two grandfathers, but Jeremy was fond of Mark's father and she used to let him visit that grandfather once in a while. Jeremy always had a good time doing that. She'd never felt free to bring him to see her own father but she figured it would work, as well.

"He's an easygoing child," Hannah continued, convincing herself as much as anyone else that the meeting between her father and Jeremy would be positive.

"I've heard he's got a vivid imagination," Mark said with a grin. "My sister said he turned her broom into a horse on the first time he visited. She couldn't sweep the floor for days because he was rounding up cattle."

Hannah looked at Mark and nodded. She wasn't sure how she felt about sharing Jeremy with him. Part of her was glad for both of them, but the other part wished the meeting between them would take place after Jeremy was well again.

*Please, God, make him well again*, she prayed as she stood there.

She was more than willing to share Jeremy with anyone who would love him, but she wanted to be sure her son was strong before she risked him gaining a father who might slight him. She knew Mark was watching her, but she didn't know what more she could add to her words.

"He likes horses," Hannah finally settled for adding.

Mark nodded. "Does he have any television heroes? You know, from the cartoons?"

Hannah shrugged. "He's not a cartoon, but he's partial to Davy Crockett."

Mark laughed in seeming delight. "A frontiersman?"

"And he loves comic books," Hannah said, smiling just seeing Mark so happy. "All of those bang-up wow characters are his favorites. The one that climbs walls like a spider and, of course, the cowboys that fight bank robbers. He refuses to go anywhere without at least a few of his comic books. He calls them his heroes."

"I used to like comics, too," Mark said. "He and I are going to have fun."

With that, Mark picked up the jar and wrapped it up in the gunny sack her father had pulled from beneath the sink.

Hannah stood there while Mark walked outside. Her father sat at the table for a few minutes before finally getting to his feet.

"I'm glad Mark is helping us," her father said as he looked at Hannah. "But I don't want you to be getting too friendly with him. You and Jeremy need someone who will be there for you and not be going off to the hospital."

Hannah frowned. "He couldn't help being in that coma."

Her father shook his head. "If it wasn't a coma, it would have been something else. The Nelson men are no good when it comes to women. They stray—even tempting good women when they do. I won't see you hurt again."

"I appreciate the concern," Hannah said. Her father

looked worried, but she didn't understand why. "Mark has always been good to me."

"He's a chip off the old block," her father said. "First it was the wild drunkenness—just like his father. Old Man Nelson used to have those blackout spells, too, when he had too much to drink. Next it will be chasing women all over town. Believe me, I know what the Nelson men are capable of doing."

With that, her father limped out of the kitchen. "I best go see he gets that part on the combine right."

Hannah just stood where she was. She didn't know what to think. Her father was bitter about something, but it had been that way since she and Mark were kids so it wasn't the robbery. Whatever it was, it wasn't fair to blame Mark for something his father must have done.

She finally moved over to the window. Her father and Mark were walking out to the combine together. It didn't look like they were talking, though. She figured the next two days would be quiet ones around here.

She reached over to pick up the receiver on the black wall phone next to the kitchen cabinet.

"Mrs. Hargrove?" Hannah said after she'd dialed the number and gotten an answer. She recognized the older woman's voice immediately.

"I'm wondering if you can bring Jeremy over to my dad's house?" Hannah asked, figuring Mrs. Hargrove wouldn't be surprised by the state of the living room walls. "My dad has a concussion and I'm watching him for the doctor or I'd drive back and get Jeremy."

"Oh, dear," the older woman said. "What happened?"

"He had a car accident," Hannah said, realizing she never had gotten all of the details. "He cracked some ribs and hit his head."

"I'll be right there," Mrs. Hargrove said. "I'll bring some of my herbal teas, too. One of them is good for headaches."

"And stay for lunch if you'd like," Hannah said.

The older woman sounded delighted and offered to bring the salad she'd planned to make for herself. "I doubt your dad has much food at his place," she added. "I know how ranchers are at harvest time."

"I better check," Hannah said as she stretched the phone cord so she could step over to the refrigerator and open it.

"You're right," Hannah said after she surveyed the few items it held. "But I see a big block of cheese and I know he has some kind of pasta. There's milk and some spices, too. I already planned to make macaroni and cheese. Jeremy's favorite. With the salad, it'll be perfect."

"I'll stop by the café and get a few of their dinner rolls," Mrs. Hargrove said. "I haven't done my usual baking this week or I'd have some of my own to bring."

"Tell Lois I'll pay for them when I come in tomorrow," Hannah said. "Although I have to say that, from what I remember, your rolls are better. The café buys its bread."

Mrs. Hargrove gave a pleased laugh. "Jeremy and I will be there as soon as we can. Charley is up visiting one of his cousins today so we're free as can be."

Mrs. Hargrove had married her good friend, Charley Nelson, when Hannah was a freshman in high school. Charley was Mark's father's cousin. The bride and groom had both been in their late sixties when they walked down the aisle, but Hannah loved the story of their courtship. She had wondered back then if she and

Mark would ever be as much in love as the two of them. She was especially touched because Mrs. Hargrove announced she would be keeping the name she'd gone by for decades because she didn't want to confuse the children of the town.

As Hannah hung up the phone, she wondered if she would ever have a romance like the one Mrs. Hargrove had. The older woman assured her it was possible if Hannah didn't give up on love. At the time she had promised Mrs. Hargrove that she wouldn't. Of course, neither one of them knew what was going to happen. Mark's coma had changed so many of Hannah's hopes.

# Chapter Four

The sun was directly overhead when Mark decided he was ready for a break. It was noon and time to eat. He'd been working for a couple of hours and the clouds had gradually scattered so it was no longer likely to rain. Hopefully that would help Mr. Stelling relax a little. The odds were improving that the rancher would get his crop harvested without any weather damage.

Mark climbed down from the combine, carrying his water jug, and saw dry wheat chaff rise around him like a fine dust storm. He sneezed. It was blazing hot and his legs were cramped from being in the same position with his foot on the gas pedal.

Mark paused a long moment and stretched as he stood on the ground. Then he pulled his work gloves off and wiped the sweat from his forehead. His hands were red from the heat. If it was like this for him, the job was too hot for someone of Mr. Stelling's age, even if the man didn't have a concussion to complicate things.

This combine was an older model than the one Mark's family used and there was no cab on it, so nothing shaded the driver from the sun. Besides, there was a rattle in the motor. This old piece of equipment wasn't going to hold together for another season.

He wondered if Mr. Stelling lacked the money to hire one of the harvesting crews that serviced other small ranches or if he was the kind of man who was just determined to do everything himself. Mark suspected the latter.

Then he glanced up at the mound of golden wheat settling into the back of the combine bin. He couldn't fault any man for wanting to feel the satisfaction of seeing his own crop harvested by his own efforts. Mark decided he'd probably never know the answer to why Mr. Stelling did anything. With that thought in his mind, Mark started walking across the field, heading to the ranch house. The older man wasn't apt to confide in him anyway.

Still, Mark made a mental note to volunteer for the next round of harvesting in the spring, as well. He walked along and stopped when he came next to the small dwelling where Hannah and Jeremy were staying. It had been a long time since Mark had given any thought to the place where the ranch hands stayed when they worked at the Stelling ranch, but it was clear the building had not been used for several years. Weeds were growing right up to the cement step that led to the front door. The white paint on the outside had turned gray and was chipped. One of the windows had been boarded over for some reason. If he wasn't mistaken, the roof had a few leaks where the shingles were curled up near the tin stovepipe that connected with the old fireplace inside.

Someone—he guessed it must have been Hannah—had stretched a red striped blanket over the window in the living room area. She had probably done it for privacy, but he wondered if the house was safe. He walked over to see if the door was locked. There was a time when no one around here worried about security, but he was no longer sure that was wise. The knob turned easily and there was no apparent keyhole, so it wouldn't be as simple as finding a new key for a lock that was already installed.

Mark walked away shaking his head. He didn't like the thought of Hannah and Jeremy staying out there. The sun baked the ground during the day and the heat hung in the air at night, so Hannah might be tempted to leave a side window open and the door ajar. There wasn't much crime around, but Mark didn't want to take any chances. He'd heard from his sister that Jeremy had a calico cat, but what this place needed was a large dog of some kind—one that would growl and bark like he meant to attack any intruders.

Mark decided that, after he finished the combining, he'd see about fixing the place up some. If there was any hardware at the ranch, he'd put a lock on that outside door before he left today. He wanted to take care of Hannah and their son. When Mark came around the corner of the main house, he noticed Mrs. Hargrove's red car was parked at the side of the driveway. That meant Jeremy was here, Mark told himself with a grin. He stepped faster and then hesitated when he got to the steps. He sat down on the top one. After opening the lid on his jar of water, he poured the liquid over his hands. Then he ran his wet fingers through his hair. He doubted any four-year-old boy would worry overmuch about farm dust, but he didn't want to get the boy's clothes dirty when he hugged him.

He stopped to consider. Come to think of it, he wasn't sure a boy that age would want to be hugged. He knew all boys went through that stage when they thought they were too old for things like that. He didn't want to push any boundaries—especially because Jeremy wouldn't know who Mark was. As far as the boy knew, Mark was just another ranch hand he didn't know.

Mark took the gunny sack off the jar and beat it against the side of the porch until the dust was gone. He'd had a glimmer of an idea about how to please Jeremy and now he thought it might be just the thing. He twisted the burlap into the shape of a coonskin cap before he started walking up the steps. Even a stranger could tickle the fancy of a child.

Mark hesitated at the door and then knocked.

"Come on in." Someone—he thought it was Hannah—called from inside the house.

Mark turned the knob and pushed the door open.

The living room was empty, and even though it was midday, shadows filled the room. He could hear voices coming from the kitchen. There was the sound of a young boy talking amid the words of the two women.

He didn't know where Mr. Stelling was, but Mark stood for a moment in the doorway to the kitchen and enjoyed the sight of Hannah stirring something in a pot at the stove. Her auburn hair was a bit mussed as though she'd stood in a steam room. Red strands of her hair sparkled in the sun coming through the window. As Hannah did her stirring, she was talking to Mrs. Hargrove. The older woman was clad in her usual checked housedress and had her hair pulled back in a serviceable bun. Over the years, her face never seemed to change. The lines in her face were from smiles and not worry. She never hesitated to speak her mind, but she was the kindest person he knew. At the moment, she was setting a plate of rolls in the middle of a table that was set for five.

His eyes went to the boy. Jeremy had a good-sized calico cat in one hand and was holding a comic book in the other. Between turning the page on the comic book and keeping the cat in place, the boy was having a time of it. He was dressed in a blue T-shirt and jeans, and his lips were pressed together in concentration. Mark was content to just watch his son, but then Jeremy turned and saw him.

The boy's eyes widened and he relaxed his grip on both the comic book and the cat. The comic book fell to the linoleum. The feline turned out to be a scrapper, though, and stood squarely in front of Jeremy. When Mark didn't retreat, the cat arched its back, preparing for an attack.

Mark wondered if his son's cat couldn't do a dog's job after all.

"Easy now," Mark whispered, not sure whether he was directing his remark to Jeremy or his fierce furry defender.

Neither of the women seemed to hear Mark and they kept talking.

Jeremy didn't seem inclined to say anything. He just looked at Mark suspiciously. Finally, Mark decided he'd tip the scales, so he put on the hat he'd just fashioned.

That only seemed to puzzle Jeremy.

"You're not Davy Crockett," the boy said, his voice clear. His thin face was serious. "I know you."

For a moment, Mark's heart soared. Maybe Hannah had already told Jeremy that he had a father. Mark was going to reach out his arms to the boy when several things happened.

The cat hissed. Hannah turned around. And Mrs. Hargrove looked up from the tomato she was dicing.

Jeremy was continuing to speak, though. "You're the man who can't wake up. I saw you in the hospital."

Mark's hopes fell. "When?"

Jeremy nodded and reached out to his cat. The feline went over and rubbed itself against the boy's legs. The cat might be fierce to others, but it was purring for Jeremy.

"I took him to see you once," Hannah said to Mark, almost apologetically. Then she stepped away from the stove with a pot holder in her hand. "I had no idea he'd remember. He was only two years old at the time."

"You came to see me?" Mark was stunned. His sister and father hadn't said anything about Hannah going to the hospital nursing home to see him. Maybe they hadn't known. He knew she'd taken Jeremy out to his family's ranch to spend time with his sister and father, but he'd never questioned if she had come to sit by his bedside.

"Just a few times," Hannah said, looking down. "And I only took Jeremy once. I couldn't find anyone to sit with him and I didn't think he would even notice where he was. I took in a few of his comic books so he'd have something to look at. Back then he couldn't read. Now he knows simple words like *bang* and *run*. You know, superhero words."

Mark wasn't used to seeing Hannah so rattled.

"It's not a problem," he assured her. "I'm pleased that you came."

He wished someone had thought to tell him something this important. Surely the nurses had known. Of course, the staff who had been there when he finally came out of his coma might have been different ones than those who had been there the first years. They might not have known how special Hannah was to him.

"I felt I should do something," she said, looking uncomfortable.

Mark suddenly realized how difficult it had been for her. It hadn't just been the pregnancy and Jeremy. All of the feelings she'd had for him had been left hanging. "I'm sorry I wasn't there for you. For us."

*For Jeremy*, he added silently.

Hannah nodded, but she still didn't meet his eyes.

"I often wished I could call you and talk or something." She raised her eyes and he saw they were damp. "Half of the time I didn't know what to do. Growing up, you always seemed to know the answer to everything."

Mark swallowed. "I wish you could have called me, too."

They were both silent for a minute.

"I thought I smelled your mother's perfume a few times," Mark finally said. Even in his coma, he could recognize scents. Hannah had taken to wearing the cologne her mother had left. "I never thought it was real— I figured I imagined the smells—but maybe part of me knew you'd been there."

He liked to think he hadn't left Hannah completely alone, although he certainly had been no comfort to her.

Hannah didn't seem to know what to say, but she did smile.

Mark felt his nerves relax as he stood there. Rays of sunshine came in through the kitchen window. Mrs. Hargrove had been standing still, but with the tension broken, she reached up into the cupboard and brought down a serving bowl.

Jeremy made a small noise and Mark looked down at the boy, who had scooted closer to his mother and leaned against her right leg. He was staring at Mark, wide-eyed. The cat stood guard at the boy's side.

"Did you smell me, too?" Jeremy whispered into the quiet. "When you were asleep and I visited with Mommy."

Mark squatted down so he could be level with his son. "You know, I did smell a cowboy a time or two. Kind of a horse scent. That must have been you."

Jeremy grinned and Mark noticed he was missing one of his front teeth. The boy's hair was a rich brown and he had a sprinkling of freckles along a round nose. His hair was nicely cut and Mark wondered if Hannah took him to a barber. After her experiences in foster homes, it was something she would do to make the boy feel self-confident.

"My grandpa has horses," Jeremy confided as he stepped away from his mother and came closer to Mark. He realized his son meant Mark's father. Mr. Stelling had Angus cattle when he had any farm animals at all. "Someday he's going to give me a ride on one of his horses. A big one, too. Not a little pony."

Mark nodded.

"'Cause I'm a big boy," Jeremy added proudly.

"You sure are," Mark said, pleased to hear his son's dream.

Mark had heard the same plans from his father's mouth. But Hannah hadn't brought Jeremy to visit the Nelson horse ranch for months—not since Mark had gotten out of the nursing home.

"Maybe I can ride with you," Mark offered tentatively. He didn't figure he would get his first hug on this visit. Although the cat hadn't advanced upon him recently and he supposed that was some progress.

Jeremy thought a moment and then his hair bounced up and down as he gave a vigorous nod. "You can put my saddle on. I'm not big enough to reach."

"It's a deal," Mark said and then he offered his hand to his son. "That's what cowboys do when they make a promise."

Jeremy beamed, shaking hands with satisfaction.

"I'll look forward to it," Mark said and then looked up at Hannah. She was still standing there, watching him and Jeremy, and looking worried.

"Is it all right?" Mark asked softly. He didn't want to add to any unhappiness she might already feel. "I won't say anything I shouldn't."

He tried not to feel disappointed that Hannah wasn't rushing to tell Jeremy that he'd just met his father. When Mark looked at her side of things, he supposed she'd thought it would be better to wait and let the boy get to know him some first.

Mark looked over and saw the compassion in Mrs. Hargrove's eyes. The older woman had seen it all. Just looking at his first Sunday school teacher reminded Mark that she always told her students prayers worked. She'd made them memorize James 5:16.

"The effectual fervent prayer of a righteous man availeth much," he softly quoted the last portion of the Scripture verse. He'd quoted that verse to her many times as a boy before he had lost his way and didn't think of prayer or God.

Mrs. Hargrove gave a slight smile as she nodded. "Sometimes the answer takes a bit of time, though."

Mark could see she was pleased. He'd had several conversations with her about prayer over the last few months. She'd been one of the church members who had organized the prayer chain when he'd been in the coma. He could never thank her enough for that. Every day for four long years, someone in Dry Creek had prayed for him. It still humbled him to remember that fact.

Hannah had learned the James verse in Mrs. Hargrove's class, as well. She recognized the spiritual moment she'd just witnessed between Mark and their teacher.

"I wish I'd taken all of your words to heart sooner in my life," Hannah said to Mrs. Hargrove. "It would have made things easier."

The older woman beamed at Hannah and she wanted to think of something more to say about her growing comfort with God. But before she found any words, she smelled something burning and instead quickly turned back to the stove. She grabbed the pan of macaroni and cheese and set it on a burner that was cool.

"I'm sorry," Hannah said. She reached over to open a window to let the trail of smoke out. "I'm usually a pretty good cook, but—"

"It'll be fine," Mark said. "Whatever it is, it will be wonderful."

"That's right," Mrs. Hargrove added.

"It's cheese and mackies," Jeremy said as he stepped closer to Mark. "Do cowboys eat black mackies?"

"Macaroni," Hannah murmured.

"All the time," Mark assured the boy. "But these

macaroni noodles are probably not burnt. They're crispy. Just the way cowboys like them, cooked over a campfire when they're out on a trail drive."

Her son was looking at Mark with a rapt attention. "Have you been on a trail drive?"

Hannah was surprised at Jeremy's ease with Mark. Her son didn't usually warm up to men very readily. But perhaps he sensed Mark's likeness to his father. His Nelson grandpa was one of Jeremy's favorite people. It was that grandpa, too, who had regularly sent Hannah money over the years to help support her and Jeremy.

"I've been some places with horses," Mark said, taking Jeremy's question seriously. "Rodeos and such. But I haven't been on a real trail drive. Maybe someday."

"Me, too," Jeremy said with confidence as gathered up his comics and walked over to the table. He set the comics on the table before crawling up into one of the chairs. Then he looked over at Mark and patted the seat next to him. "Sit here. Beside me."

Hannah watched Mark sit down in the chair next to Jeremy just as her father came into the kitchen. He'd been in his bedroom changing clothes since he'd gotten a few drops of blood on his harvesting shirt in the accident earlier. She knew that garment reminded him of her mother, so Hannah thought he might also want to spend a few minutes in quiet talking to her mother's photo. He used to do that a lot and she hoped he still did.

"I smelled something," her father said as he stood beside the table.

Jeremy was sitting in the chair Hannah's mother always used. Her father never used to let anyone sit there and Hannah saw him hesitate. Finally, he must have decided it was all right because he walked over and sat at the head of the table where he generally sat. He didn't even complain about the ragged comic books Jeremy had set by his plate.

Hannah scraped the macaroni and cheese out of the pan and into the serving bowl Mrs. Hargrove had brought down from the cabinet. The food was a little more burnt than crispy, but Hannah had tasted it and it seemed edible. Besides, Mrs. Hargrove had made a large salad with lettuce, tomatoes and cucumbers so they'd do fine.

"Oh, I forgot," Hannah said, suddenly remembering. "Lois sent us out a chiffon pie for dessert. Apparently one of her key lime ones was damaged and couldn't be served."

She had checked the box when Mrs. Hargrove had first laid it on the counter. Hannah was prepared to pay Lois for the pie if it wasn't a reject like she claimed, but Hannah agreed with the other woman's assessment. The chiffon had a gash in it where a knife had fallen while Lois was apparently cutting something else.

"I think we must be the chiffon pie capital of the world," Mark said as he eyed the box. "I asked Lois once and she makes twenty of the pies each week. Some key lime. Some lemon. A few strawberry."

"They're popular," Hannah said as she pulled her chair up to the table. "Lois says she thinks she could sell twice as many."

Her father snorted. "Of course she could. All of the ranch hands around here are sweet on her. Half of them buy a whole pie just to keep the others from having a piece and talking to Lois while they eat it. One of these days that woman is going to have to pick one of those boys. A woman that age should be married."

Hannah tried to tamp down her irritation. "She's only fifteen or so years older than I am. I don't see any reason for a woman to rush into marriage."

Her father sobered up. "Having a young son is reason enough for any woman to marry. Who's going to take the boy fishing?"

Hannah glared at her father. "I can fish."

"You grew up in the city 'til you came here," he said, scoffing. "You don't know anything about fishing."

Hannah stared at her father. Surely he'd taken more note of her than that.

"I taught her to fish," Mark said. His voice was mild as though he was hoping to avoid conflict.

Her father scowled. "When was this?"

"We were probably ten years old," Mark said. "Maybe eleven. Shortly after she moved here."

"Mom was still alive," Hannah added. She knew where this was going. "She said it was okay. I had permission."

"It was a fool thing to be doing," her father muttered, but he seemed chagrined. He stared down at his plate.

"It would have been nice to have gone fishing with you, too," Hannah said quietly.

"I was busy," he said curtly.

"I know," she said.

Then she held out her hand to both her father, who sat on one side of her, and to Mrs. Hargrove, who sat on the other. "Dad, would you pray for us?"

Hannah saw the shocked expression on her father's face. He looked up and around as though he was searching for an escape. It suddenly occurred to her that prayers might not still be said in this house. He had said the blessing with every meal before.

"Maybe Mrs. Hargrove can," her father finally mumbled. "She's a visitor and all. Good woman."

"It's a privilege to pray," Mrs. Hargrove said with a nod. Then she bowed her head.

Hannah closed her eyes. She wondered if her father had always been out of his depth when dealing with her. Maybe he meant to be a more active parent. He must have initially agreed to welcome her into his family. The adoption agency wouldn't have proceeded if he hadn't. But then maybe God had intended for her to come to Dry Creek regardless of what her father thought. The Bible was full of stories like that.

Hannah let the calming tones of Mrs. Hargrove's words comfort her and she sat there. It was the first time she'd considered that God might have wanted her to come to Dry Creek for any other reason than to be a daughter for the Stellings. Maybe she did have a bigger place in His plan than she'd known. What that might be, she couldn't imagine. Maybe He just wanted Jeremy settled here for a few months while he underwent treatment for his leukemia. She still wasn't sure how to tell him that he was so very sick. Whatever she was going to say, though, she needed to get the words in hand soon.

## Chapter Five

The temperature had fallen and it was dark by the time Mark reached the end of a row of wheat and shut down the machinery. He'd worked as long as it was safe. The headlights on this combine were weaker than those on later models and, when all traces of twilight had faded from the sky, there was not enough light to see much in the field. Hannah had flagged him down some hours ago to tell him she was driving back to Dry Creek with Mrs. Hargrove to get her car. Then she handed up a couple of sandwiches. He'd eaten, but he was weary.

So tired, in fact, he almost stumbled as he took the final steps up to the house porch. A light shone in the kitchen and he knocked lightly on the door. It had to be past ten o'clock and he didn't want to startle anyone. He waited a few minutes before trying again. He was beginning to think Hannah had left the kitchen light on by mistake when he heard soft footsteps in the living room.

"You're done," Hannah said as she opened the door. Her hair had been loosened from her ponytail and the denim shirt that covered her T-shirt looked rumpled, like she had been sleeping in it. Relief was evident in her voice. "It's completely dark out there."

Mark nodded as he stepped inside. "Not even any stars out, which means there's still clouds. It might rain tomorrow. I wanted to get as much done as I could."

"My dad and I are grateful," she said, looking a little shy.

"I'm glad I can help."

Hannah smiled. "I'm happy you were here, too. I've had a hard time getting my dad quieted down enough to rest. He's that worried. And then I have to wake him up every few hours and make sure he's all right. That doesn't help him relax."

"Does he seem okay, though?" Mark asked. He figured it would take more than a knock on the head to damage Mr. Stelling too much, but it didn't pay to take chances.

Hannah nodded. "I checked in with the doctor this afternoon and he said my dad should be well enough tomorrow to go over to Mrs. Hargrove's with Jeremy while I work my shift at the café. She offered and I hate to leave my dad alone. He'll complain about it, but—" She shrugged. "It's for his own good."

Mark's eyes were adjusting to the shadows in the living room and he noticed the pillows and blankets on the sofa. "And have you gotten any sleep?"

The light from the kitchen was gradually outlining everything.

"I didn't want to miss thanking you," she said with a yawn. "And I thought you might be hungry. I can make a grilled cheese sandwich for you and I found a couple of cans of vegetable soup in the cupboard. We ate most of it for dinner, but I saved a bowl back for you."

Mark had noted her tiredness and was going to decline the offer, but his stomach growled.

Hannah grinned. "I guess that's a yes." She turned to walk toward the kitchen. "It'll only take a minute to heat up the soup."

"That sounds good," Mark said. "My throat will appreciate something hot after all the dust. But I can go into the kitchen myself and fix it."

Hannah had reached the doorway to the other room and she looked back. "After all you've done, you deserve to just sit there and rest for a few minutes."

Mark admitted the idea of leaning his head back on the sofa sounded tempting. The house was silent as only a place of sleep could be, and he was tired of the noise that old engine had made all afternoon. He wished he'd asked what room Jeremy was sleeping in so he could go peek in and see his son as he slumbered. It was probably Hannah's old room, he decided. Mr. Stelling wouldn't want a child sharing his space, and Hannah probably wouldn't allow it, either, since that would mean Jeremy would wake up every time she went to check on her father.

Mark's breathing slowed as he felt the tension of the day leave him. He wasn't aware of starting to doze, but it happened. He wasn't even sure how much time had passed when he felt a soft breath coming down on his face. For a second, he wondered with joy if Hannah was planning to kiss him. But then he felt two things at the same time. Little fingers started to pry his eyelids open and a cat jumped on his lap.

"Ah," Mark gasped involuntarily.

He opened his eye and saw Jeremy's face a few

inches away. He was peering at Mark's left eyeball. "Can you wake up?"

"I'm fine," Mark whispered. He wasn't sure why he kept his voice low, but he figured Jeremy was supposed to be in bed and Mark knew he'd like to have a few moments with his son before the boy needed to go back to sleep.

"Really, I'm good," Mark said softly when Jeremy didn't move.

Finally Jeremy settled down by the cat, both of them making themselves comfortable on Mark's lap. The cat even started to purr.

"I thought maybe you couldn't wake up again," Jeremy confided as he snuggled close to Mark.

"Like when I was in the hospital?" Mark asked.

The boy gave a slight nod.

"You don't have to worry," Mark assured him. "I'm all better now."

Jeremy seemed satisfied and Mark congratulated himself on his parenting skills. He'd navigated those questions pretty well, he thought, for a brand-new father.

Mark was content sitting in the semidarkness of the room when he heard Jeremy sigh.

"Still worried?" Mark asked.

"I have to go to the hospital, too," the boy said, his voice heavy. "My mommy won't tell me, but I know."

Every nerve in Mark's body woke up. He wouldn't make any sudden moves since he didn't want to scare Jeremy, but he needed to know what his son was talking about. Maybe the boy didn't really mean what it sounded like, though.

"Are you going to visit someone?" Mark asked

gently. "Like when you and your mommy came to see me that time?"

Jeremy shook his head. "I'll be by myself. Mommy doesn't know I heard her talking to the doctor."

The boy sounded desolate. "I think I can take my comics with me because they're small," he added as though it was the one bright note. Then his head dropped. "The doctor said Callie can't come. Cats aren't allowed in the hospital."

"That's—" Mark cleared his throat, but his voice still didn't make it through.

"I wish I was a cat," Jeremy said and rested his head against Mark's chest. "Then I wouldn't be allowed to go there, either."

Mark wrapped his arms around the boy. He had to include the cat in the hug, but he was willing to do that to hold the boy. The feline didn't seem to view this indignity favorably, but maybe she was as worried about Jeremy as Mark was because, after one skeptical growl, the beast settled into the hug without too much fuss.

"I'm glad you're not a cat," Mark whispered and then kissed the top of his son's head. "I've never seen a cat ride a horse."

"Me, neither," Jeremy said as he sat up straighter.

The hug had fallen apart by that time, but Mark figured it had done what it needed to do. Jeremy was looking better. The cat stayed on Mark's lap. The reason became clear when Jeremy's hand reached over to bury itself in the animal's fur.

They were quiet then, just sitting together in the shadows and breathing. A few seconds later, Mark put his hand on his son's back and rubbed. He remembered his mother doing the same thing to him when he was sleepless as a child.

As he saw Jeremy's eyes droop and then close, Mark realized he could sit here like this all night long. He was a father. He had a responsibility. Nothing had ever felt so good. Someday soon, his son would know who he was. All of the prizes that he'd ever won didn't compare with the feeling inside his heart at this moment. He had two people to protect now—Hannah and their son. A man could not ask for more, he thought as he vowed to himself not to fall short on the task. He'd be there for them this time.

Hannah stood in the doorway and stared. Enough light came from the kitchen to show her what had happened. The sofa with its sagging cushions was along the wall next to her, and in the middle of it was a scene that would break any single mother's heart. Jeremy had his elbow wedged into Mark's chest, and her son's head was pressed against his shoulder. The look of bliss on her son's face was the same one he'd worn the day she'd given him permission to bring the cat home.

She wished she could buy her son another pet instead of having him cozy up to Mark. She loved her son without reserve, but she did not know how to protect him. She had decided this afternoon that she needed to keep Jeremy distracted when Mark was around so that her son wouldn't become attached to him. And now it looked like it was too late.

His heart would be broken. Mark liked to win—at sports, in school, in everything. She feared that Jeremy's leukemia would prevent him from scoring any victories when it came to those kinds of things. Mark might be polite to her son, but she doubted he would be there to push a boy in a wheelchair or console him if he stumbled when he tried to race and came in last.

It was a pity, Hannah thought as she walked over to the sofa.

"Jeremy," she whispered as she reached out and touched her son. "You're supposed to be in bed."

Jeremy looked up, his eyes unfocused, but still lit with joy.

"Mommy," he said and lifted his arms to her.

She gave him a hug as she scooped him up.

"You'll be a sleepyhead tomorrow if you don't get to bed," Hannah said as she cradled her son's head with her hand.

"I'm fine here," Jeremy protested as his weight sagged against her. "I can stay on the sofa."

"You need to be in your own bed," she said and then looked around and spotted the cat sitting at Mark's feet. Hannah knew the feline couldn't be comfortable. Of course, Callie would never leave Jeremy's side when there was a stranger around and Hannah was glad for the animal's watchfulness. "Callie won't be able to sleep beside you unless you go lie down."

Jeremy wiggled so he could see his cat, but he made no further protest. Hannah let him settle in for a few minutes before she looked over Jeremy's shoulder and met Mark's eyes.

"I'm sorry," she said. "I know you're tired."

"I'm glad he woke me up," Mark said.

He sounded sincere, Hannah thought as she carried her son out of the room. Callie followed, but Mark sat there watching them all leave.

She slipped Jeremy into his covers and then walked

back to the living room. She was surprised to see that
Mark hadn't moved to the kitchen.

"Your soup will get cold," she said. "I set it on the
table for you. The sandwich, too."

"I know you've had a long day, as well," Mark said.
"But I'd like to talk for a few minutes."

Hannah knew instinctively that something was
wrong. Her mouth went dry. "Do I need an attorney?"

She had dreaded this talk with Mark. She's read dozens of accounts of divorce proceedings and talked to
as many single mothers. Jeremy was her son, but she
knew she didn't have enough money to fight the Nelson family if they decided they wanted to take custody
of him. She knew there was no reason for her fears.
Neither Mark's father nor his sister had ever indicated
they would do something like that. And, in all fairness,
the Mark she used to know wouldn't take advantage
like that. But she was afraid nonetheless. Anyone who
looked at her history would find out she knew nothing
about raising a child. She hadn't even seen family life up
close until she came to Dry Creek, and then she felt like
she was outside looking at something through a window.

"No attorneys," Mark said, and she felt the breath
she'd held leave her.

"It's about doctors and hospitals," he said instead
as he stood up.

"Oh." That was its own set of problems. She looked
over to make sure Jeremy wasn't sneaking out into the
hallway. He wasn't. She turned back to Mark. "We
might as well go into the kitchen. You can eat while
we talk."

The light felt subdued when Hannah stepped back
into the kitchen. The bulb had a yellow cast to it and

the whole room looked older than it did in the daytime. She supposed her father had forgotten to buy the regular bulbs and used one they kept for the barn. She had scrubbed and mopped the tile floor after Mrs. Hargrove left, though, so that looked adequate, at least.

"I've tried to keep all the places clean where Jeremy and I live," she said to Mark. She was aware that if she didn't it would be points against her in a custody battle. "I can't always afford the best apartments around, but I make sure they're neat. Jeremy is past the stage of crawling, but I use disinfectant on all the floors where I can. And I clean the carpets."

She sat down at the table, opposite where she'd laid the dishes out for Mark.

"You work too hard," Mark said as he slid into the other chair.

For the first time, she noticed the red color on his face. She supposed the shadows had hid it until now. "You weren't sunburned when you came in at noon."

"I know," he said. "The sun came on strong about two o'clock. And the chaff didn't help. Some of this is windburn."

"My father should have some salve for that," Hannah said as she started to rise. "It'll be in the medicine cabinet."

"The burn doesn't hurt," Mark said. "I'd rather eat first, if that's okay. I do want to talk."

She sat back down.

Mark looked at her for a moment and then held out his hand. "Would you mind praying with me before I eat?"

She reluctantly took his hand. She could hardly refuse to pray with someone, but she worried it might take the edge off her resistance. And she sensed there was more to come in this conversation. Still, when Mark bowed his head, she did as well.

"Father," Mark prayed. "We are grateful for all Your provisions for us today and we ask Your guidance as we go forward into tomorrow. We ask that You protect Hannah's father throughout the night and be with our son. We ask these things in Jesus's name. Amen."

"Amen," Hannah said and opened her eyes.

She was relieved to see that Mark was looking down at his soup.

"This smells good," he said with a smile as he reached for his spoon.

He ate with relish and Hannah relaxed. "My father doesn't keep much in the house for food, but Lois said she'd arrange for me to get some groceries tomorrow."

"Nothing wrong with a bowl of vegetable soup," Mark said as he scooped up the last bite. He'd already eaten the sandwich. "I'll bring some fresh fruit over from our house when I come in the morning. Jeremy could use some oranges."

Hannah wrapped her arms around herself. She knew what was coming.

"Is there anything else he needs to be eating to get well?" Mark asked. "Milk? Eggs? Just let me know and I'll get it."

Hannah shook her head, blinking away her tears.

"It's not about food," she said. "He's a precious boy. He worries about other people—"

"He sure was concerned about me," Mark said with a grin. "I've never had anybody check my eyeballs before. Not even in the hospital nursing home. I'm wondering what is wrong with him."

Hannah smiled back even though she could feel the

tears starting to fall down her cheeks. "I don't know how it happened, but the doctor says Jeremy has leukemia."

Mark went still. The grin dropped from his face.

Everything was silent.

"Did you say leukemia?" Mark finally asked.

Hannah nodded. "Some kind of a cancer. Not very many kids get this kind—six thousand a year around the country—and it took some time for our doctor at the time to find it. This was when we lived up next to Canada on the Hi-Line. At first, the doctor thought it was some kind of flu. But Jeremy just got weaker and weaker. Finally the doctor did enough tests to find it. He suggested I take him to a specialist in Billings."

She stopped, but Mark didn't say anything. He was looking at her intently, waiting for her to finish.

"We went just the once. It was the specialist who found not only the leukemia, but also a tumor in the bone of his leg." Hannah stopped to reach in her pocket, searching for a tissue. She wiped away her tears. Then she started to hiccup. She didn't know why, but every time she started to cry she ended up with the hiccups.

"Let me get you a glass of water," Mark said as he stood up and walked over to the counter. He reached up into the cupboard and brought down a glass, then filled it at the faucet.

When he brought it back to the table, he set it down. "Here you go."

By this time, the hiccups were so deep that they were painful. Hannah reached for the water and had a hard time bringing the glass to her lips. She couldn't control the tears any longer.

Mark reached out and steadied the glass as she

drank. The cool water soothed her throat. She finished the glass and Mark held it. Then she laid her face down on the top of the table. She heard the sound of Mark setting the glass down and then felt his hands start rubbing circles on the middle of her back. He used to do that when they were kids and she got her hiccup attacks. There was nothing that helped to ease them better.

She looked up and he enveloped her in a gentle hug.

They stayed like that for five or so minutes. By then the hiccups were completely gone. She wasn't inclined to move, though. Her emotions were spent. She hadn't told anyone else about the leukemia, and she realized it had been hard for her to carry it alone inside her. She didn't want Jeremy to have people worried about him, though. He was a sensitive child and he'd know something was very wrong if that happened.

She felt Mark kiss the top of her head.

"You haven't told Jeremy, have you?" Mark asked softly. He was so close, his hand was still on her back and his face was only inches away.

Hannah shook her head. "I figured we should go to our meeting with the doctor on Wednesday before I say anything. I won't be able to answer Jeremy's questions until then anyway."

"The doctor in Billings?"

"Yes," she answered. "They have a children's cancer center there and they do experimental treatments. The leukemia is a kind that they can treat, but the tumor in the leg is something else. It's unusual. I read about a stem cell treatment that can be done to help with the leukemia and the tumor, but I'm not sure if our insurance will cover it. The procedure hasn't been approved for regular treatment yet, but this cancer center has done it many times."

"I'd like to go to the doctor with you," Mark said.

Hannah lifted her head. She hadn't thought this through. "I don't know."

"I'm his father," Mark said. "Maybe I could be a donor or something for this stem cell treatment—if that's what he needs."

"I don't know that much about it yet," Hannah said. Their doctor had it in his charts, but she realized she didn't know Jeremy's blood type. Of course, that likely wouldn't affect stem cells anyway.

"We'll figure it out together," Mark said. "You've got tomorrow to think about it. Today's Monday."

Hannah nodded. She'd be able to make a better decision after she had some rest. She wished she could foresee how long Mark would be willing to be involved with Jeremy if their son was sick.

"You know Jeremy might not be able to walk very well," she cautioned him. She looked for any reaction.

Mark paused. "I hope it doesn't come to that for him."

Hannah tried to decipher that response and she couldn't. He didn't look like he was thinking of distancing himself from Jeremy, but she didn't know yet. "We'll talk more tomorrow."

Mark stood at that point. "You're tired."

She nodded. "Totally beat."

"I'll see you in the morning, then," he said. "That's if I get here before the rest of you leave for Dry Creek."

"Sounds good," she said.

"Oh, and I want to fix the door on the small house after I finish the combining," Mark said. "I might do some painting, too. Before you go in the morning, put your stuff someplace where I won't get anything on it."

"Almost everything is still in the car," she said as she stood, as well. "Do whatever you want in the house. You can't hurt anything."

Mark nodded and started walking toward the living room.

"I'll let myself out," he said. "Lock the door behind me."

Hannah watched him leave. Part of her wanted to go with him, even though he was only going over to his family's ranch. She had not felt so alive in the past four years except—she paused and remembered. It was different, but she'd loved Jeremy, and her days with him were some of the most precious she'd had in her life. She could not afford to be distracted by Mark, not when she had Jeremy to worry about. She was glad she'd told Mark how sick their son was, but she was the one who was ultimately responsible. She was the mother and Jeremy didn't even know he had a father.

Hannah sighed. That was another problem and one she wasn't ready to face tonight. At some point, she would have to tell Jeremy just who his father was. Even after the cozy scene she'd seen tonight, she wasn't sure how her son would feel about having a father.

## *Chapter Six*

Mark drove his pickup onto the Stelling ranch a little before six the next morning, Tuesday. It was still dark outside so he couldn't see enough of the sky to judge whether it would rain or not. What he did know was that he had to finish the combining as soon as he could. He had passed Hannah's car outside Dry Creek when he was coming this way. Glad to see her, he stopped to roll down his window and say good morning.

Hannah greeted him, but looked distracted and said she needed to get to work. She had her father tucked into the passenger seat and a sleepy Jeremy in the back seat. Even the cat had left the ranch for the day and was curled up on Jeremy's shoulders. Mark suspected his son was using the cat as a pillow, but the feline didn't seem to mind.

Mark decided now was not the time to ask Hannah if she had decided whether he could go with her Wednesday when she took their son to the doctor. She had her hair pulled back in a ponytail and her red T-shirt on. Her eyes were not puffy from crying so he figured she was okay. He wished her well and she drove away. Mark could hear a rattle that told him her old car needed a tune-up, though. He'd add that to the list of things he'd do once he finished the harvesting.

"She won't find me so easy to send away," Mark said aloud as he squared his shoulders. No one was there to answer him back, but it didn't diminish his satisfaction. He liked doing things for her and he intended to do them.

He had known when he left his family's ranch that he'd be too early to go out into the fields, but he'd come over anyway so he'd have time to work on the lock for that small house. He'd rummaged through the tack room in the Nelson barn last night and found a used lock and key combination that he thought would work. They had obviously been taken off some broken-down door decades ago, but locks hadn't changed much in all that time and, as far as he knew, keys were ageless.

Just knowing some things stayed the same made him feel optimistic about the future. He hadn't been left behind that much after being in limbo for those four years.

He was whistling as he pulled his pickup to a stop beside the main house and stepped down. Some twenty minutes later, he had the lock on the door and was trying the attached key when he heard a pickup pull into the yard. He stuck his head out and saw Randy Collins walking up to the main house. Randy was the only paid wrangler on the Nelson horse ranch and, since it was Tuesday, he was likely on his way into Miles City for ranch supplies.

"Hey!" Mark called as he stepped out of the house so he could get Randy's attention. "I'm over here."

The other man changed course and started walking toward Mark. "I'm glad to see you."

Mark noticed Randy's limp was giving him some trouble. A medium-sized man, the cowboy was bow-legged and as plain as they come. His face was clean-shaven, but had a flatness about it that made him look sturdy rather than handsome, especially when he wore his usual Stetson. Randy instinctively knew how to get a horse to do what he wanted, though, and he was loyal to his friends. In short, he was an old-fashioned cowboy.

Mark patiently waited for the other man to get within easy talking distance. There was no sense in them yelling at each other across the empty yard.

"Lois—" Randy managed to say when he arrived. He was breathing hard from hurrying. Mark knew he meant the waitress at the Dry Creek Café since she was the only Lois around. Besides, Randy had had a crush on the woman for over a year now and was, in his mind, subtly courting her.

"She asked if I would get some groceries for Hannah and her boy," he said once he got his wind back. "I stopped as the café was opening. Hannah gave five dollars to Lois, who gave it to me."

Mark figured Randy was making it clear that he wasn't doing the favor for Hannah. The man knew how Mark felt and wouldn't want to put himself forward with a woman Mark had strong feelings for.

"Hannah said she wanted some kale and popsicles," Randy continued. "Red and purple. The popsicles, not the kale. And a couple cans of tomato soup."

"That's it?" Mark asked incredulously. "That isn't enough to keep the two of them fed, and then there's Mr. Stelling, too." Mark pulled out the wallet he kept in his shirt pocket and handed two twenty-dollar bills to Randy. "Get them a package of hamburger meat and some vegetables. Maybe apples, too," he added.

Mark wasn't sure what his son should be eating, but everyone said apples were good for you. "Maybe carrots for vegetables and a few big potatoes for baking." He paused. "Didn't Hannah say she wanted anything else? Kale isn't enough to make a meal."

"I offered to give her the chiffon pie I'd ordered for today," Randy said, his broad face pinking at the words. "Lois made a lemon one. That's her specialty."

"You ordered the whole pie?" Mark asked and then grinned. He knew it was the entire thing because Randy had been buying as many of Lois's pies as he could. "Afraid some of the hands from the other ranches will come in and buy a piece?"

Randy shook his head. "I wouldn't mind if they bought some pie, but they all seem to want to sit around and talk to Lois while they eat it." He was silent for a minute. "The truth is, I'm getting kind of tired of chiffon pie. I always preferred apple anyway."

Mark knew that fact from the pies stacked in the refrigerator in the bunkhouse that he and Randy shared. "Wouldn't it be easier just to tell Lois how you feel?"

"I'm working up to it," Randy said defensively. "A man can't just go up and ask a woman to marry him without some…time."

"Maybe not, but you could ask her out to dinner," Mark said.

All of the pink had drained from Randy's face and he looked white. "She might say no." His voice was low. "She hasn't said yes to anyone else and she's been asked. Lots of times. And if she won't say yes to Jacob

Marsh—and him all duded up in that new Western outfit of his—what chance does a man like me have?"

"Well, then, just—" Mark started and stopped himself. He realized he had absolutely no idea what Randy
should do. In years past, Mark would have suggested
winning a rodeo or dazzling a woman with some fancy
moves on a dance floor. Back then, he'd outshone Jacob
Marsh. Not that Mark ever really wanted anyone but
Hannah. Still, he was popular at dances and he'd heard
rumors of girls who wanted to date him.

"Just be yourself," Mark finished.

"That's what I'm being," Randy protested. "Steady
and slow."

Mark nodded. He wasn't sure that was a winning
strategy, but he didn't want to discourage the man.
"Well, she'll like it when you get groceries for Hannah. Did you bring one of the freezer bags?" The grocery store was in Miles City so when they bought ice
cream or anything frozen, they needed to zip it in an
insulated freezer bag and put it in a cooler with ice so
it would arrive in Dry Creek without melting.

"I've got one in the pickup," Randy said with a nod.
"For the popsicles."

"Well, you're ready, then," Mark said.

Randy just stood there a minute.

"I just wanted you to know I'm not moving in on
your girl," Randy finally said as he turned to go. "Your
Hannah is real nice, but it's Lois for me."

"Thank you," Mark said as he watched his friend
walk away. He wondered if Lois even knew what she
was missing by not noticing Randy. He was a good,
solid man who would treat a wife like a queen. But then,

maybe Lois did want someone with more style. For all he knew, she was holding out for a banker. Or a doctor.

Mark marveled that he'd ever thought he'd known anything about romance. He'd never courted Hannah. They'd been such good friends that the other feelings just sort of snuck up on them. He wondered now if that hadn't been a mistake. Maybe if they'd officially dated they would have something more defined when they did come together.

As he listened to Randy drive his pickup away from the Stelling house, Mark turned and started walking back to the small house where Hannah and Jeremy would be staying now that Mr. Stelling didn't need to be awakened every few hours. Mark should be getting out to the field, but he intended to wash the one window in the run-down place that wasn't boarded over.

He turned the light switch on when he stepped inside the little house this time. Some boxes and suitcases were piled in a corner of the living room. There was no furniture. He hadn't realized that Hannah didn't have much, but she had said she moved everything in her car and there was not a lot here. Maybe she'd sold everything before she left her old place. He did notice a deflated air mattress that she must have used that first night she'd stayed here.

He decided he would go over to his family's house after he finished the harvesting and bring back a cattle truck loaded up with whatever he could find. There were pieces of furniture in the attic that hadn't been used in years. He was sure there were a table and chair set up there and a double bedstead. He'd find a mattress to go with it if he had to bring the one off his own bed. In the meantime, he'd take care of that window. It looked like it hadn't been washed in years and it made the inside of the house look gloomy.

When Hannah left the café at three o'clock her feet were tired, but she'd had a good day. The café was open for dinner only on the weekends so she hadn't had to work late, but business had been brisk for lunch. She always felt better when a café had enough customers that she knew her work was required. She'd quit a job once because she found out the owner was keeping her on as an act of charity after business declined. Fortunately, that wasn't the case in Dry Creek. She could barely keep up with the requests for pieces of lemon chiffon pie. She'd been surprised it was so popular with the ranch hands around here. But Lois said they always came in for lunch just so they could have her pie. When she'd lived here, Hannah remembered the work crews from the ranches eating out of a hot thermos and having a sandwich, but she supposed things changed even in a quiet town like Dry Creek.

Fortunately, Hannah did not have to drive far to pick up Jeremy and her father. Mrs. Hargrove's two-story house, surrounded by a sturdy white fence, was only a quarter of the mile down the paved road from the café. Of course, nothing was far from anything else in this town. There were no sidewalks. The whole of Dry Creek wasn't more than a dozen clapboard houses, the café where she worked, a hardware store and a church. The gas station was past everything else on the opposite side of town and she'd heard rumors that someone had bought the old Keifer place down the road and was turning it into a cozy bed-and-breakfast.

She remembered as a teenager that everyone in

her class at school complained nothing ever happened around Dry Creek. She'd nod her head when the others said this, but secretly she was glad. She'd already had enough happenings to last a lifetime by then. She soaked up the peace.

She parked her car along Mrs. Hargrove's fence and got out of the vehicle. Her favorite place in this town had always been Mrs. Hargrove's kitchen. It had a row of paned windows with white ruffled curtains. One summer she'd helped the older woman make chokecherry jelly for a whole week. Hannah had never had so much fun, squishing the juice out of the cooked berries, making labels for the sparkling jars of preserves and then tallying up the final count.

The older woman must have been listening for her because she opened the front door of the house before Hannah even got partway up the walk. Mrs. Hargrove had a butcher's apron covering her checked housedress and her gray hair was twisted into a serviceable bun. She's gained some weight since Hannah had lived in this tight-knit community, but she still seemed to bustle when she moved.

"Did you have a good day?" the older woman asked with a smile on her face. She had stepped outside and closed the door behind her.

Hannah noticed that the smile didn't reach the other woman's eyes.

"Is something wrong?" Hannah asked.

"I'm worried about Jeremy," Mrs. Hargrove said, her voice little more than a whisper. "But I didn't want to say anything where he could hear me. Children are so sensitive about things like that."

Hannah braced herself. She knew what was coming.

Worries had swirled around in her head all day while she worked. Last night, Jeremy had seemed more frail than usual.

"Most boys his age don't want to take a nap," Mrs. Hargrove said. "But he not only went to sleep willingly right after an early lunch, he slept so long I thought I should wake him so he'd be ready when you came. But it wasn't easy to do. I think something might be wrong."

Hannah took a ragged breath. She hadn't told anyone except Mark, but she couldn't keep it in any longer. "There is. The doctors think he has leukemia and also a cancerous tumor in the bone of his leg."

"Oh, dear," Mrs. Hargrove pressed her hand to her mouth briefly. "The poor boy."

"I'm taking him to a specialist in Billings tomorrow," Hannah said. "The local doctor where I used to live finally made the diagnosis, but he said they have experimental treatments that might make a big difference. This specialist is supposed to be the best one in the whole state. I'm counting on him to know what to do."

The words had spilled out of Hannah in a torrent and she didn't realize until she finished that Mrs. Hargrove had stepped close and enfolded her in a hug. The older woman smelled of cinnamon and roses.

"I'm going to pray for you both right now," Mrs. Hargrove said in Hannah's ear, and then she began to call down God's mercy on her.

Hannah didn't recall having anyone ever pray for her in such low, soothing tones. She felt warm all over. The older woman talked to God like He was standing right beside them, and Hannah liked to believe He was. Mrs. Hargrove had always told her Sunday school classes that God loved them deeply and was in the room with them.

Hannah had to blink when Mrs. Hargrove said her "Amen."

Then the woman stood looking at her. "Is your father going with you to the doctor?"

Hannah shook her head. "He doesn't know about Jeremy. And he's not really too comforting when someone's sick."

"I know." Mrs. Hargrove pursed her lips. "He had a hard time when your mother died. But you need somebody with you. I have a doctor's appointment myself, but I can cancel it and—"

"No," Hannah said. "You've already done so much. Jeremy and I will make out fine."

"But what if the doctor wants to do some tests on Jeremy?" Mrs. Hargrove asked. "The boy might need someone to hold him in the back seat while you drive home."

"I hadn't thought of that," Hannah said. The older woman was right. Any number of things could happen. After all, the doctor had recommended she have some popsicles on hand for when Jeremy got home from the appointment. It was one of his favorite treats. "Don't worry. I do have someone to go with us."

Hannah hadn't decided until just this minute to accept Mark's offer, and it left her feeling breathless.

"Lois?" Mrs. Hargrove asked, still looked troubled.

"No." Hannah shook her head. "It's Mark Nelson."

Relief flooded the other woman's face. "That will be fine, then. He'll see to everything."

It didn't take long after that for Jeremy and her father to come out to the car and climb in. Her father had carried out the box of groceries that Lois had arranged to have her friend Randy pick up for them in Miles City.

"That can't all be kale and popsicles," Hannah protested when she saw how heavy the box was.

"It's not," Mrs. Hargrove said. She'd come out on the porch carrying a small ice chest. "Mark Nelson had asked Randy to add a few things to the box—which we kept refrigerated so it's all cold. And this is for the popsicles."

"But I didn't give him enough money," Hannah protested as she automatically took the cooler. "He can't have gotten all this."

She was sure she'd seen a couple of packages of meat and a carton of milk.

The older woman shrugged. "You'll have to talk to Mark about that. Randy said everything was paid for."

By that time, her father had already stowed the box in her trunk, so there was nothing to do but to set the ice chest back there, too, and take it all home with them.

The gravel roads spreading out from Dry Creek were dusty and Hannah drove slowly. These were the kind of roads not meant for speed. Besides, she was in no hurry to get back to her father's place. He would not need her to watch over him tonight, and she hadn't had time to fix up the small house where she and Jeremy would be staying. She didn't want her son to be surrounded by ugliness on the night before his doctor's appointment. She would have to think of something.

She had a couple of comic book character sheets for his bed. Maybe she could hang them over the walls. She kept thinking her son would find new cartoon characters to enjoy, but he seemed to stick with the same old-fashioned ones. She had begun to wonder if this was good or bad. Maybe he was afraid to look for new heroes.

## Chapter Seven

Mark stood back and admired the wall he'd just painted. He had finished harvesting the wheat around noon, and when he'd gone back to his family's ranch to get something to eat after that, he made another trip to the barn's tack room and found an assortment of cans of paint left over from the time his sister painted the kitchen and the downstairs bath. Between trims and accent paints, he had five or six colors. He'd come back to the Stelling place and cleaned the window in the small house. Then he scrubbed the cigarette smoke stain off the walls in the living room. By the time he finished the last wall, the first one was dry, so he went to work with the paintbrush.

He had two coats of yellow on one wall and a partial pattern on half of the ceiling before he heard the rattle of Hannah's car. The window he'd just washed faced west and the sun was shining through, so when he turned to look, he saw Hannah clearly. He stepped out in front of the house and waved so that everyone would know where he was. His pickup was still parked at the main house. When Hannah went to her trunk, he remembered the groceries and hurried across the weedy ground.

"Let me carry those," he said when he got there. By then she had the car trunk open and she was reaching for the boxes.

"I can get it," Hannah said as she put her hands through the hand holes in the box.

"Of course you can," Mark said as he stood to the side until he saw her falter. She couldn't lift it. So he put his hands under the box, as well. "Things are always heavier than they look."

She let him take the whole thing. "You know, I plan to pay you back for whatever money you gave to Randy this morning."

He heard Jeremy and Mr. Stelling as they walked to the main house. Mark glanced up enough to see that Jeremy was dragging his feet. Mr. Stelling held out his hand and helped the boy up the steps to the porch. The cat was following them into the house.

"Jeremy's tired," Mark said as he looked over at Hannah.

She nodded, looking weary herself. "I can't seem to manage anything these days."

"Of course you can," Mark protested. "You already got him to a doctor who diagnosed him and you're going to take him to a specialist tomorrow."

"I forgot my money at home today or I would have had more to give Randy for groceries," she confessed. "I should thank you for covering for me."

"Did he say I gave him any money?" Mark asked Hannah. He knew very well Randy would not say anything of the sort.

"No," Hannah admitted.

"Maybe they just had a sale at the store," Mark said. "Or maybe he had some coupons. You can save a lot that way."

Hannah leaned over and looked into the box he held.

"There's a whole chicken in there," she said. "Not to mention a package of hamburger meat and a couple of cans of tuna fish."

"And apples," Mark noted when he looked down. There were also carrots, potatoes and an onion.

Hannah must have kept looking, because she turned to him. "All of the ingredients for some chicken soup."

"That should build up Jeremy some," Mark said. He'd have to thank Randy for adding a chicken to the box. "That's what my mom always used to make when any of us were sick."

"Mine did, too," Hannah said, looking more positive than she had earlier.

"See, you'll do fine," Mark said as he hefted the box so it settled against his hip and started to walk to the door that Mr. Stelling had left open. Hannah picked up the small ice chest and carried it beside him.

Mark was suddenly conscious of how much parenting Hannah had been forced to learn on her own while he had been laid up with that coma. He wished he could make up for some of it. His father told him he'd regularly sent money to Hannah to help her with Jeremy, but Mark figured it hadn't been enough. He planned to sit down with her and set up a schedule of payments. Of course, that would be only the beginning. His childhood hadn't been perfect, but he wanted to be a good father to Jeremy. He wasn't sure of everything that would mean, but he planned to find out.

* * *

Once she was in the main house, Hannah put a blanket over the window in the back bedroom so that Jeremy would be able to take a nap. He came willingly when she called and she tucked him in. He was asleep before she left him lying there. His cat was curled up at the bottom of the bed and she expected it would doze, too.

On the way back to the kitchen, Hannah passed the living room, where her father and Mark were discussing the wheat crop. She caught enough of the words to know that her father was pleased with the careful job Mark had done with the combine. Mark had also called someone to truck the wheat to the closest grain elevator. She thought she had smelled the wheat dust when she walked into the house minutes earlier. She remembered that from her childhood.

Hannah told herself things were getting better as she put the chicken in the oven to roast for supper. Her father didn't have much more than salt and pepper in the cupboard, but she coated the bird with a little olive oil and applied what seasonings she had freely. She'd hold back some of the cooked chicken from the table tonight so she could make a pot of soup for tomorrow, too. It made her feel good to cook, like she was sharing this kitchen with her mother again. She was glad Mark had reminded her that her mother had always made chicken soup, saying it would cure whatever ailed you. She knew it wouldn't cure Jeremy's leukemia, but she hoped it gave him some comfort and feeling of home.

"Mommy!"

A sharp cry came from the back bedroom. She hurried to her son, but she had to go through the living room, and by the time she got through the doorway, Mark was already heading down the hall.

When Hannah reached the bedroom door, she saw Jeremy with his arms wrapped around Mark's neck, looking like he'd never let go. Her son had been frightened. His breathing was still ragged. That cat of his paced the floor by the bed as though she disapproved of Jeremy seeking comfort from a stranger. Hannah couldn't blame the animal for that; she felt the same.

"Mommy," Jeremy called again—his voice softer this time—and Hannah went to him, sitting on the bed next to Mark.

She expected her son to fling himself into her arms. After all, she'd been his sole comforter since he was born. But Jeremy didn't seem inclined to loosen his death grip on Mark. What her boy did instead was cling to Mark's neck while he rested his head against her shoulder with what looked like extreme relief. Hannah had to reach around Mark to pat her son on the back, but that's what she did.

"Sorry," Mark whispered, sounding reluctant as he started to untangle himself from Jeremy's grip. He looked over at Hannah. "It's you he wants. I just got here first so he figured any port in a storm."

"I'm glad you were here," Hannah murmured as she held her hands out to her son.

Jeremy did give up Mark then and came to her. She saw the flash of loss on Mark's face. Whatever happened, she was beginning to understand that Mark did want to be a father to her son. She might have to work on trusting him whether she wanted to or not. She didn't want to cause Jeremy any distress and her son seemed to have become attached to Mark the moment he met him.

She was still troubled by the longing she saw on his face when he looked at Jeremy curled up in her arms.

"We'll have to tell him soon," she said, sharing the task with Mark the only peace offering that she could think of.

"Not now, though," Mark said, although he looked pleased at her words. "We can wait until things settle down. He's had enough to deal with today."

Hannah nodded. Jeremy burrowed into her arms the way he used to when he was a toddler. She started to rock him and she felt him relax until he went soft.

"Bad dream?" she asked him.

Her son nodded. "It was dark in here. I thought I was asleep."

She probably shouldn't have covered the window, Hannah thought. He was usually fine without light when he slept, but maybe that was because she was always in the room with him. She wasn't so sure she'd sleep well without his breath on her face, either.

"I'm sorry, baby," Hannah murmured as she drew Jeremy closer.

When some time had passed, Mark stood up from the bed and said he should get back to the work he had been doing in the small house. He wanted to finish more of it, he said, before the sun went down.

Her father, who had come to stand in the doorway, frowned as he watched Mark get up. He must have forgotten how pleased he was to have his wheat harvested because he scowled at Mark and then declared he had some phone calls to make before he stomped off.

"He's just—" Hannah tried to think of a believable reason to excuse her father's rude behavior, but Mark interrupted.

"Don't worry about it," he said.

"I can't help that," Hannah said with a half smile.

Mark looked at her, his eyes lingering on her mouth. "Come with me."

Jeremy must have been listening to Mark because he climbed down from Hannah's lap, ready to leave.

Hannah stood, intending to go chop up something for supper. But then she remembered her father and decided she should give him some privacy since the only place in the house with a phone was the kitchen. So she nodded toward Mark and, taking Jeremy's hand, walked beside Mark through the living room and out the front door into the heat of the afternoon. She noted the sky was clear so the threat of rain had passed.

"What I'm doing isn't finished," Mark cautioned her as they neared the little house.

Hannah was conscious of all the weeds in the dirt as they walked. The crop might be taken care of with the help of Mark, but the yard around here needed work. This yard used to be covered with cultivated grass and now there was nothing but clumps of the strongest wild grass that blew through and lodged in every nook and cranny in the spring winds. It didn't look like her father made any effort to keep the property up. She knew Mark was talking about the house, but she already knew the same longtime neglect would be found there.

"Anything you've done to the place will be an improvement," Hannah answered. Jeremy was walking between the two of them, holding one hand from each of them. He sounded like he'd forgotten his earlier distress. He seemed to enjoy holding both their hands, but Hannah figured he would not be able to keep his balance on this rough terrain without the two of them. The cat, as always, followed in her son's wake.

Hannah surveyed the land again, looking at it with a new image in her head.

"You couldn't get a wheelchair over this," she muttered, almost to herself. Everything would tip over and Jeremy would spill out.

Hannah had barely made a sound, but Mark must have heard her. He stopped in midstride and turned to face her.

"Is that what you're expecting?" he asked in a tone just as soft as the one she'd used. "Is that what the doctor said would happen?"

"Oh." She wished she'd held her tongue. Mark looked appalled at the thought of a wheelchair. She wasn't sure how he would feel about Jeremy if her boy ended up in one of those things. Half of the doctors she'd talked to said it might happen that way, especially with the complication of a tumor.

Hannah looked down and saw her son look up with a curious expression on his face.

"It's nothing," Hannah finally said loud enough for everyone to hear as they started walking again. "Nobody needs to worry. I was thinking of…using it to deliver our groceries."

She saw the jaw on Mark's face tighten, but he didn't say anything.

Mark opened the door wide when they got to the house, and Jeremy dropped both of their hands and stepped inside. Mark touched Hannah's arm before she could enter, too.

"I'm not worried about me," Mark said in a low, tense

voice. "Don't treat me like I'm on the other side. I'm not. I want what is best for Jeremy."

Hannah looked up. She'd have to be blind not to see that he was sincere.

"I didn't want him to know what we were talking about," she admitted. "He might be scared."

Mark grimaced. "We need to learn to speak in code like other parents do."

"Oh," Hannah said. She felt a butterfly flitting around in her stomach. "I've never learned how to do that."

"We used to speak in code," he said. "Remember?"

"But we were spying then." She grinned at the thought. "The cows were enemy soldiers and we had to get across enemy lines."

"That didn't last very long," Mark replied. "I can't remember why."

"You had football," she said. She'd had a fierce wish to be a boy about then. They'd been in the sixth grade. She'd been devastated not to be able to join the team. She was glad they let girls join now. "You said you didn't have time."

"Well, that was a shame," he said. "We would have gotten good at all those dots and dashes we used. After all, we had the cows fooled."

"They weren't even paying us any attention," she said.

Right about then, Hannah heard a whoop coming from inside the house.

"It's a hero's room," Jeremy exclaimed when Hannah stepped inside. He turned to her with a wide grin on his face. She hadn't seen him so happy since the last time he'd been able to pet a horse.

Hannah looked forward, seeing the room through her son's eyes.

The bright yellow wall had a sparkling clean window square in the middle and rays of afternoon sun were pouring through, filling the whole room. A strip of ceiling above the wall was painted blue and a series of comic features popped out from the blue. She recognized Davy Crockett and the superhero with the cape. There was even an angel with a sword standing on a cloud and what looked like Cupid in the corner.

"You won't have to worry about the darkness anymore," Hannah said to Jeremy.

He nodded vigorously. "They won't let anyone get me."

"Who's going to get you?" Mark squatted down to ask him.

Jeremy just shrugged.

When it became apparent Mark wouldn't receive a response, he stood up.

Hannah looked over at Mark. "Thank you."

Jeremy turned then and added, "Thanks from me, too, Mr. Man."

"You're most welcome," Mark said, his face losing its serious expression and eventually beaming at both of them.

"I'm going to go look in the kitchen," Jeremy announced as he started to walk toward the other room.

"I haven't done any work in there yet," Mark called out a warning as the boy went through the doorway.

Hannah felt a sense of peace watching her son explore new territory. Then she turned to the other wall.

"Oh!" she exclaimed with delight.

A solid-looking double bed, with a curved mahogany headboard and a firm mattress, was lined up with that far wall. A white blanket and several white sheets were folded on top of the mattress. She could see right away that a person, even a little boy, could lie in that bed and look through the window, pretending he was having adventures with his comic book heroes.

"Where did you get the bed?" Hannah turned to Mark. She knew she and Jeremy would have a good night's sleep in that bed. There were even new pillows. The air mattress she'd brought with her didn't stay inflated throughout the night, and when she used it, she had to add air about one o'clock in the morning.

"The headboard belonged to a bachelor uncle of mine at one point," Mark said. "It's been in the attic at our house for as long as I can remember."

"It's an antique!" she exclaimed, her enthusiasm waning. "Oh, I couldn't use something like that. It's hard to make sure Jeremy doesn't jump on the bed and I wouldn't want to damage it. I couldn't replace it."

"Jeremy can pound away all he wants," Mark said with a grin. "All of the legs have been replaced at some time or other. And there's a crack on the back of the headboard. I doubt if it would bring more than ten dollars in an auction." He lifted his hand. "And the mattress is clean, but it's old. No antique at all. So, no, you can't pay me for any of it."

Hannah blushed. She had just been going to say she would give him the ten dollars when she collected some more tip money. She'd bought a good mattress some years ago, but she'd never owned a bed frame before and she wouldn't mind buying it outright. She had always rented furnished apartments and the furniture had never been good. One time she and Jeremy had to share a single bed and the headboard on that had been nothing but heavy cardboard.

"I only hope you both are comfortable enough sleeping on it tonight," Mark continued. "I found another mattress, but I'm going to look through some more things in the attic and see if I can't find another bed frame, so you'll want to use the second mattress then. I'll bring a table and chairs over tomorrow when I come—"

Hannah stiffened.

Mark stopped and studied her. "I thought I'd come over around six o'clock in the morning."

She felt foolish for reacting so she only nodded.

Everything was silent for a few minutes.

"Will that give us time before we head off for the doctor's appointment?" Mark said with his face suddenly stoic. "Have you decided if I can go with you? I'm happy to do the driving."

"Yes." She was relieved to share her decision. "Mrs. Hargrove was determined that I get someone to go with me. She said I needed someone."

"Well, she's right," Mark said as his face relaxed. "I'm glad we have that settled. Nobody should have to go through something like that alone."

She was going to nod again when she saw Mark suddenly look stricken. She wondered if he'd changed his mind about going with her to the doctor, or maybe he remembered another commitment he'd made and couldn't go.

"I am so sorry," Mark said, his eyes locking on hers. "I just realized that I don't even know all of the times you felt alone when you were pregnant with Jeremy. You must have gone to the doctor several times. I hope you didn't have to go alone. And then when Jeremy was born and you had a baby to take care of—that must have been difficult. I've been planning to increase the monthly payments my father sent to you, but that won't ever make up for not being there during those years."

"Your father sent me enough." Hannah gave him a curt nod. She was suddenly overwhelmed. "Besides, I'm used to being alone."

She thought Mark would take comfort from her words, but he seemed even more distressed when he heard them. "I don't want you to ever feel like you have to face life alone again."

She didn't know what to say. Things would happen in life. "It's nice to know you want to be there for me."

That was about the best she could do, and Mark seemed to accept that because he only nodded.

"I will be here tomorrow," Mark finally said. "I can bring my pickup to drive or borrow my sister's car if you'd rather we use that."

"Which one has the biggest back seat?" Hannah asked. "In case we need to stop and take a break for Jeremy. We could pull into a rest stop and he could take a nap if he's tired. He doesn't have much stamina these days."

"My pickup would be wider," Mark said. "And I think it's longer, too. Plenty of room. Are you going to bring those comic books of his? Since he can't have his cat, he'll want the comics."

"He will, won't he?" Hannah figured she should have thought of doing that earlier, but it was nice to have someone else looking out for Jeremy. "Thanks for thinking of it."

"Jeremy's the one who thought of them," Mark confessed. "But we make a good team—you and me. We always have."

Hannah couldn't deny that. They had survived everything together as children and then young teens. She was beginning to hope they could be friends again. She could probably handle being friends with Mark if she didn't rely on him too much. It was all a matter of balance, she told herself. And then she looked at him.

*Lord, help me*, she prayed.

# Chapter Eight

It was still dark when Mark pulled his pickup into the yard of the Stelling ranch. He could tell by the air that the day was promising to be warm and dry. There were no lights on in the main house, but he saw a dim one in in the window of the small house, which meant Hannah and Jeremy were likely up. He figured they would not have eaten yet, but it didn't matter because his sister had packed them a bag of pumpkin muffins. She also set him and Hannah up with a thermos of hot coffee and one of cold grape juice for Jeremy.

Mark dimmed the lights in his pickup and turned the ignition off. Swinging his door wide, he stepped down and began the short walk to Hannah's door.

Hannah answered the knock with her hairbrush in her hand and a worried look on her face, and then she whispered, "Do you have gas in your pickup? I should have reminded you that the doctor is not in Miles City, he's in Billings."

She'd opened the door only partially. He supposed that was so their words would not carry inside.

"I'm good," Mark assured her softly. She was dressed

in denim jeans with a pink sweater over a white cotton blouse. "Have you told Jeremy yet that he's going to the doctor?"

She shook her head. "I don't want to scare him."

*That's why she doesn't want our words overheard,* Mark told himself.

"He probably already suspects." Mark felt he could say that much without betraying Jeremy's trust. "He's a bright boy."

"I'll tell him soon enough," Hannah said defensively.

Mark was silent for a moment. Then he remembered suddenly that she had said she'd taken Jeremy to the doctor in northern Montana where she lived and the man had some difficulty in even diagnosing the boy's leukemia.

"You moved here for the doctor, didn't you?" he asked.

She nodded and then added, "I need to get Jeremy up. I thought I'd let him sleep as long as we could. He's been tired lately and, if the doctor does any tests today, I want him to make a good showing."

With that Hannah opened the door fully and stepped aside so Mark could enter. Most of the room was in shadows, but Mark could see the lump under the covers on the bed.

"Let me wake him," he said. "It will save you time."

"That would be great," Hannah said as she turned toward the kitchen. "I need to get my hair up and put a pot of coffee on." She stopped and looked around her, a little disorientated. "I forgot my coffee maker is still in a box somewhere."

"That's okay," Mark said. "Allie fixed me a hot thermos full of coffee. We can each have a cup as we drive. She packed us some muffins, too. Pumpkin ones."

"Bless her." Hannah flashed him a smile. "Jeremy loves her pumpkin muffins. He's always telling me I need to make some, but I don't have the recipe. I was going to get it from her."

"I'll make sure you have it," Mark said. He would reach up and pluck down the evening moon if Hannah said she wanted it. A recipe was nothing. But Hannah looked pleased.

"I also have some grape juice for Jeremy," Mark added.

"I'll bring a sippy cup so he doesn't spill it," Hannah said as she stepped into the kitchen. "I need to call my dad, too, before we go and make sure he's up. He should be out of the danger zone with his concussion, but I need to check anyway."

When she was gone, Mark turned toward the bed. Jeremy hadn't stirred and they hadn't been that quiet. He wasn't sure about the boy's normal habits, but most children of his age would bounce out of bed at the slightest noise.

Mark sat down on the bed. He noticed Hannah had put a pillowcase covered with pictures of horses on the pillow that their son clutched in his sleep. Next to the pillow were several comic books. Mark reached over and gently shook the boy's shoulder. Jeremy made a few sleep sounds and then rolled over.

He was pale, Mark thought as he studied the small face. And he had a blue tinge to his skin. Mark leaned closer and decided maybe the blue was just from the morning shadows. He pulled back, shaking his head. He wondered how anyone managed to be a parent. So many alarming health things could go wrong with a child and there was no real protection against most of it.

Mark bounced slightly on the mattress and the springs moved with him.

Jeremy's eyes opened slightly. The boy rolled over and pulled the blankets over his head. Mark put his hand on the boy's back.

"Time to get up, son," he said and then caught his breath. He'd spoken without thinking. He knew Hannah didn't want to spring the news on Jeremy this way so he tried to keep his voice even as he said some more. "We need to get going soon. Billings is a long way to go and we don't want to have to hurry."

He was babbling now, Mark knew, so he forced himself to stop. After a few minutes, he realized silence was not a good strategy. Then he looked up and saw that Hannah was standing in the doorway from the kitchen with a look of horror on her face.

She had obviously heard him call Jeremy his son. Mark shook his head slightly so she wouldn't speak. Then he tried to think of something to distract the boy just in case he had been listening more carefully than Mark thought he had been.

"We might drive by some horses on the way to Billings." He knew at least one ranch on the way that had some fine saddle horses. He looked up at Hannah. "The Clarke ranch. It's a bit off the freeway, but not impossible. I know one of the wranglers there. He'd show us what they have."

Jeremy peeked out from behind the blankets, his eyes lit up with interest.

"Maybe on the way back," Hannah said. "I don't want to be late for—" Her voice faded.

"Of course not," Mark agreed. Hannah had too many secrets from their son, but he didn't want to upset her.

He glanced down. Jeremy had pulled the covers back over his head and, if Mark hadn't caught the look earlier, he'd think the lump in the bed had not moved. He put his hand over Jeremy's foot. The boy didn't pull away and Mark took that as a good sign.

"I have pumpkin muffins in my pickup." Mark was careful not to mention who had made the muffins just in case Jeremy was able to piece together family relations and make the connection that, if Allie was Mark's sister and Jeremy's aunt, the two of them might be father and son.

Mark's bribe seemed to be working because Jeremy pulled the blankets down so his face showed.

"Do they have raisins in them?" the boy asked anxiously. "I like raisins."

Mark nodded. "They sure do. Just the way you like them."

A slow smile spread across Jeremy's face. "Can I eat the muffin in my bed?"

"We need to leave pretty soon," Mark said. "You can have a muffin in the pickup."

Mark knew he was in trouble when the boy didn't move to get out of bed.

"It will taste just as good in the pickup," Mark tried coaxing the child.

Jeremy didn't even answer.

Finally, Mark looked up at Hannah. She was still standing in the doorway watching.

"Help," Mark mouthed the word to Hannah. He wasn't facing Jeremy so the boy wouldn't see him. Mark had to admit, though, that he was out of his league. His son might only be four years old, but he was stubborn.

For the first time, Mark realized just how much he

had missed in the years when he had been away from Jeremy. Hannah might have had the full load, but Mark hadn't had the chance to learn about parenting in slow stages. He was thinking now that he might have met his match in his son.

Fortunately, Hannah was there and she silently walked over to the bed. Mark stood up so she could sit by their son.

Hannah knew better than to force Jeremy. He'd always had a mind of his own. He could be gentled, though, and she reached out to stroke his head. "I thought you liked those pumpkin muffins."

"I do," Jeremy admitted.

Hannah could tell he was wavering.

"Billings is a nice city," she continued. By now Jeremy had inched a little closer to her. "And we could go have ice cream when we're there."

Jeremy's forehead was furrowed with a frown now. She thought he would ask whether they were going to see a doctor. She was ready to tell him. Then he scooted closer still and sat up to put his head next to her ear.

"Is the man going, too?" Jeremy whispered to her.

Hannah was surprised. Doctors were not on her son's mind. She had thought Mark and Jeremy were getting along well together. Maybe she was wrong, though. She looked up and saw Mark watching them intently. He knew something was going on. She realized she didn't want to hurt him and he would be if Jeremy didn't even want to be around him. But it was her son's choice.

She leaned down so she could whisper back to Jeremy. "Do you want him to come?"

Jeremy gave a vigorous nod with his head.

"Well, then," Hannah said in relief, "you need to get up and get dressed. I laid your clothes out in the bathroom. Be sure and brush your teeth, too."

Her son nodded again and climbed out of bed. He padded in his slippers down the short hall and into the bathroom. Within seconds, she heard water running and the sounds of the chair being pulled close to the sink.

She stood up, feeling competent. She expected Mark to congratulate her.

Mark was frowning slightly, though.

"That whispering," he said. "Were you telling him that he's going to see a doctor?"

"I was going to," Hannah said. "But…he's never liked doctors or hospitals or anything medical. Maybe he doesn't need to know quite yet."

"Won't it just be more upsetting to him when he finds out where he is?" Mark asked.

Hannah had never had anyone challenge her parenting skills. It might just be that they were sympathetic to her plight and didn't want to discourage her, but not even Mrs. Hargrove had ever suggested she do something different and, if anyone had that right, it was the older woman.

"Do you think you could do it better?" Hannah asked coldly.

She had to keep in mind that Mark could sue her for custody of Jeremy and a judge might see him as the better parent. After all, he had a part interest in a family farm. He had financial stability. A sister and a father Jeremy already knew and liked. All she ever had was a month-to-month apartment and a week-to-week paycheck in a series of rural cafés. She'd never even had a steady babysitter until she moved back to Dry Creek and got the offer from Mrs. Hargrove.

Mark hadn't answered, so she repeated herself, "Do you think you could do better?"

"Of course not," Mark said. He looked sincere. "I don't think I could have done nearly as well as you obviously have with him. He's a wonderful, well-adjusted boy."

Hannah felt the irritation drain out of her.

Then Mark added, "It's just that, at some point, he has to know."

Hannah had to be honest. "That worries me, too. I just can't—" She wasn't sure why, but then it came to her. She could not add to the burden her son carried. She felt every anxiety he had, even if he could not name them. She saw the worry in his eyes and it pained her. She didn't want him to feel the aloneness she'd known as a child. The sense that he was an outsider and that disaster might strike at any time. She wanted to protect him from the whole world and she was only one person.

By then Jeremy came back into the room where she and Mark stood. The boy was dressed, but his T-shirt was on backward and he was carrying one shoe. The other shoe was on his right foot.

"I can't find my sock," Jeremy complained as he held the shoe up to Hannah.

"You sit on the bed," Hannah directed her son. This much she could do for him. "I'll go find the sock."

She needed a couple of chairs for company, she told herself as she walked down the hallway. She didn't like to sit and visit with someone on the bed, especially when they had an empty bedroom down the hall. But chairs would have to wait until another day.

The sock was in the bathtub and she returned to the living room with it in time to see Jeremy showing Mark the comic books he wanted to take with them to Billings.

"I'll need to stop on the way out and knock on the door to my dad's house," Hannah said. "I tried calling him when I was in the kitchen and he didn't answer. He might have the ringer down on his phone, though. I know he used to do that when he didn't want to be disturbed."

Mark tied a knot in the plastic bag that held what looked like half a dozen comic books.

"I'll knock if you want," he said. "I'm already used to his language when he's crossed."

Hannah had Jeremy on her lap and she was slipping the last sock onto his foot. She looked up at Mark and grinned. "I'd appreciate that. If he can string together any kind of a sentence, we can assume he's still doing fine."

By the time they were all out the door, the sky was pink with the sunrise. She had taken a blanket to wrap around Jeremy so he'd be comfortable. She saw that Mark had borrowed the car seat his father used when Jeremy visited them on the ranch. She had forgotten to mention that to Mark.

After they got Jeremy tucked into the back seat, Mark walked the few yards over to Hannah's father's house. Mark had to knock several times before he got a response, but Hannah had no trouble hearing her father's words even though she was seated inside the pickup.

"Cover your ears," Hannah said as she looked back at Jeremy. He was already nodding off, his head drooping as he sat in his car seat. He had a comic book clenched in one hand. He wasn't listening to anyone.

Mark opened the door on the driver's side and pulled himself into the cab. "I told your father we'd bring him a few bitter lemons from Billings." He looked over at her and grinned. "He said to go ahead. Said we could try and sweeten him up, but he doesn't think it will work."

Hannah shook her head. "Nothing will work if he doesn't want it to."

Mark drove the pickup out of her family's yard and onto the gravel road. When they had found a steady pace, Hannah leaned down and picked up the larger of the two thermos bottles.

"Want a cup of coffee?" she asked as she unscrewed the top lid of the cylinder. She drew in an appreciative breath of the aroma and then turned to Mark. "You be sure and thank Allie for this. I'm not sure I could have faced today without a cup of coffee."

"Pour me one, too," Mark said. "We have an extra cup in the bag."

Hannah gave the lid cup to Mark; he set it in the beverage holder by his door. Then she reached down for the blue plastic cup and filled that with coffee, too.

She figured she'd hold the cup until the coffee cooled off a little. As she sat there, though, she felt the insecurities of the day press in on her. Maybe she hadn't wanted to tell Jeremy about this visit because she couldn't hide her stress. This new doctor might give them very bad news and she wasn't ready to hear it. The doctor who diagnosed Jeremy had not gotten things right for several months. The man had her dosing Jeremy with vitamins and the boy kept failing. She hated to think what the specialist would tell her today. She almost stopped breathing when she faced her fear. She was afraid Jeremy was dying and there was nothing she could do to stop it.

Hannah blinked back tears and then suddenly realized that she had been sitting with the cup of coffee in her hand for so long that it had gotten lukewarm.

She could sense Mark looking at her and she glanced up to see him. "You going to drink that coffee or just hold it 'til it turns to dust?" Mark asked.

"I was just thinking," she said as she put the cup to her lips and took a swallow. She winced involuntarily. "Would it really ever turn to dust?"

Mark shook his head and then slowed the pickup down. "Toss the stuff out the window and get yourself a new cup."

Hannah did that. It was surprising what a good cup of coffee could do for someone in the early morning hours.

She turned to Mark. "Thanks. I feel better already."

He nodded. "Be sure and eat a muffin, too. Allie put all kinds of healthy things in them. We've got a lot of miles to cover."

Hannah nodded. She needed to remind herself that Mark was not the enemy. Not once had he suggested that she was doing anything wrong except for not warning Jeremy about the doctor. And maybe he was right about that. She just didn't know how to tell her son he was ill. She wished she was the one who was sick, but then who would take care of Jeremy?

She glanced over at Mark. Legally, if she could no longer care for Jeremy, the job would fall to Mark. Maybe he did need to spend more time with Jeremy.

# Chapter Nine

Mark was relieved when he saw the cliffs that the locals called the Rims. They signaled the entrance to the town of Billings, Montana. The three of them had made good time and would be waiting in the reception area for Jeremy's appointment. He glanced back in the mirror to see the boy. Jeremy had eaten two muffins and they'd stopped for a hamburger about a half hour ago. He'd dozed off several times during the trip, but he was awake and alert now. Mark noticed the boy had kept his comic books beside him the entire trip. He hadn't fussed, either.

"I brought some quarters for the meter outside the doctor's building," Hannah said. "They told me when I made the appointment that parking was limited and it was best to be prepared for the meters."

Mark nodded. He was glad he'd come with Hannah. She was vibrating with worry so tightly that he wondered how she would have made it on her own. But at least she wasn't pretending anymore that nothing was bothering her.

The avenue was wide that led to the doctor's office,

and Mark had no trouble finding the single-story brick building. Young trees lined the street in front and it was close to a larger building marked as a cancer center. Hannah was wise to be prepared with quarters because they did have to park on the street.

They walked up to the building three abreast. Jeremy was between Mark and Hannah. None of them were holding hands. A side door had the doctor's name and they entered the receptionist area. Mark guided Jeremy toward a row of chairs while Hannah went to the counter to talk to the clerk there.

Hannah was shaking when she came back to sit beside Mark, and he put his hands over hers to steady the both of them.

"They want to talk to me alone first," she said. She glanced down at Jeremy and then back up to Mark. He could see her force the stress from her face. "Probably just so I can fill out some forms," she said with a tiny laugh. "You know how that is."

Mark's heart went out to her. "Jeremy and I will hold down the fort." He looked over at the boy. "Won't we?"

The boy looked paler than he had yet this morning, but he nodded.

"It'll be okay, Mommy," Jeremy said, and Mark thought Hannah would start to cry. But just then a nurse with a clipboard called Hannah's name and led her into the back of the office.

"I just hope it's not about money," Hannah whispered as she passed in front of Mark.

He reached out to stop her. "I thought you had insurance."

"Deductibles," she stopped to mumble.

"And experimental stuff," she added and then kept on walking.

Mark just sat there. He almost wished his father hadn't spent so much of the ranch assets on Mark's nursing home care. The coffers were low at home and he was entitled to only a percentage of what was there. Years ago, when he'd wanted money, he'd sign up to ride in a rodeo. He wondered frantically if he could manage a win in any of the categories today.

Finally, he noticed that Jeremy was sitting very still.

Mark leaned down. "Everything okay?"

Jeremy looked up. "Is my mommy sick?"

"No." Mark was surprised. "No, she's fine."

Mark knew that Hannah should have told Jeremy what was going on, but as Mark looked at the troubled boy, he faced the same problem that Hannah had. He didn't know the words to use, either.

"It's me, then," Jeremy said, his tone defeated.

"What do you mean?" Mark asked carefully, looking down at the boy. Mark didn't want to make any mistakes. "It's you, what?"

Jeremy stared up at Mark.

"Me that's sick," Jeremy finally said.

When he had made his announcement, Jeremy stopped looking at Mark. Instead, the boy faced the reception counter, his hands gripping those comic books like the heroes inside could leap off the pages and rescue him.

"It's kind of scary, isn't it?" Mark asked quietly.

Jeremy nodded his head vigorously, but he didn't say anything. He did, however, scoot closer to Mark.

"The first thing to know is that the doctor wants to make you better," Mark said, putting his arm around

Jeremy. "And the doctors are very smart. They'll do everything they can to make you well."

Jeremy seemed to think about that for a minute.

"Will I go to sleep?" he asked then.

"You mean with anesthesiology?" Mark replied and then realized Jeremy did not know the term. "They do put you to sleep if you have an operation. I don't know if you will have one or not yet."

"I can't have one," Jeremy looked up, protesting in great distress. "I might not wake up."

"Oh, don't worry." Mark wondered where the boy got his terrors. "The doctors make you come out of it."

Jeremy stared at him, his fears not lessening. Mark noticed the boy looking down at those comic heroes in his hands.

"Nobody could wake you up," Jeremy mumbled, his head still turned down. "When you were in the hospital. The doctors couldn't do it then. Mommy asked one of them."

"Oh." Mark felt the air pushed out of him.

"Mommy tried to wake you up, too," Jeremy continued. "But she couldn't. The doctor said nobody could."

His son's voice had gone from terror-stricken to sad, and Mark scooped the boy up from where he sat beside him and settled Jeremy in his lap. Sometimes, words alone were not enough.

"I didn't have an operation," Mark spoke low for Jeremy's ears only. "You don't have to worry about not waking up because of what I had. I had a coma. It was my own fault. I did something stupid. That won't happen to you."

His son looked up at him with uncertainty written all over his face.

"It won't happen to you," Mark repeated. "I promise. You won't go to sleep and stay that way for a long time like I did."

*God help us*, Mark prayed silently so he wouldn't scare his son.

For the first time, Jeremy relaxed against Mark's chest. Mark didn't loosen his arm around the boy. In fact, he tightened it. Mark wondered if he should have promised what he could not guarantee, but it was the only thing he could do. He relied on God to protect Jeremy.

Mark sat there in the middle of the day in the doctor's waiting room and wondered how parents without faith could face the future—not the future for themselves, but for their children.

He looked up in time to see Hannah walk through the door. Her face was white and she headed straight for him and Jeremy.

Hannah sat down and reached for her son. She was on the verge of tears and she never cried, at least not willingly. Mark lifted Jeremy off his lap and settled him on hers. Only then did she start to breathe evenly. She lifted her hand and smoothed down the cowlick on Jeremy's head. He was precious to her. She looked up and tried to give Mark a reassuring smile. She could tell right away that he was as shaken as she was.

Finally she looked down and cuddled Jeremy to her. "The doctor wants to examine you," she murmured to her son. Mark had been right, she thought. She should have been open with Jeremy earlier. "I don't want you to be frightened or anything. I'll be there with you the whole time."

"I know I'm sick," Jeremy said.

Hannah nodded. She was so shaken she must have not heard her son correctly. "It's all right. I'll be with you."

"I'm not afraid." Jeremy leaned forward a little.

"Oh," Hannah said, studying her son for any signs of distress. He appeared to be sincere. "Well, you shouldn't be. The doctor wants to help you get well. He's our friend."

She said the last words a little woodenly, but Jeremy did not seem to object. He didn't seem to be paying attention.

"He—" Jeremy kept his voice private, but he nodded at Mark. "He said I wouldn't go to sleep forever. Not like he did."

"No," Hannah said, stung by his statement. He had shared his fears with Mark and not her. "No, you don't have to worry about that."

She hadn't known her son was afraid. She should have explored his feelings more when she realized he didn't like hospitals. It had to be that visit to see Mark when he was in the nursing home. It was the only time Jeremy had been inside anything like a hospital.

"Do you have any other questions about being sick?" she asked. She still didn't know what to tell Jeremy, but she could answer his concerns.

He just shook his head.

"The nurse will call us in shortly," she continued with her hand on her son's arm. "Then we go into a small room where the doctor will talk to us. He's happy to answer any questions you can think of."

The doctor had been willing to discuss all of Hannah's concerns, too; she just hadn't liked all of the answers he gave. His office had been in touch with the insurance group that Hannah used for her and Jeremy. She knew it wasn't the best coverage; it didn't sound like it would be even adequate.

"I want some water," Jeremy announced suddenly and slid off her lap, standing on the floor. "Can I get some there?"

He pointed to the big water dispenser with the little cups that were shaped like cones.

Hannah nodded her head. Jeremy always liked cups of any kind and he might as well have the thrill of drinking from a paper one.

"Did the doctor ask about your insurance?" Mark asked quietly when Jeremy reached the water station.

Hannah nodded and blinked back tears at the same time.

"I need thirty thousand dollars," she said, unable to keep the distress to herself. "For just our part."

She heard Mark's gasp and was satisfied that he was as surprised as she had been. She'd known, of course, that there would be an extra charge since the stem cell treatment that would save Jeremy's leg wasn't covered fully.

"The doctor told you it was that much?" Mark asked.

"He agreed it was unusual," she said. "But I'm not asking for the recommended treatment. Plus the stem cell is experimental and insurance doesn't usually cover those kinds of things."

"Well, what is the recommended treatment?" Mark asked.

She flinched just thinking about it. "Amputation."

"Oh," Mark replied.

"The doctor said they are primarily worried about

saving his life," Hannah said. "There are prosthetics to replace a leg. And people live normal lives with them."

"I'm sure they do," Mark said. "I've seen people adapt to almost everything in the nursing home."

Hannah nodded.

"Is there any risk to doing the stem cell?" Mark asked. "I mean, if that doesn't work, will they still be able to amputate? We'd not be putting his life at risk, would we?"

Hannah looked up. "Of course not. I wouldn't even suggest doing it if it wouldn't be safe. I just—" She paused, trying to find the right words.

"We should be able to afford to take care of our son," Mark explained it perfectly. "Parents ought to be able to do that much."

She nodded. "I don't want to have to explain to Jeremy someday that I could have saved his leg if I'd had the money."

"We—" Mark gently corrected her words. "We'll tell him you and I could have done it if we'd had the money."

Hannah turned to Mark. He looked wretchedly sincere.

She nodded. "We'll tell him we—" Then she paused. "I don't suppose you have thirty thousand?"

"If I did, I'd hand it to you right now," he said. "I have a few thousand and that'll go into the pot. Would they take a down payment?"

Hannah shook her head. "I already asked. They need the money up front."

The two of them just sat there in silence watching Jeremy walk back toward them. He was carefully holding the little paper cup in his hand.

"I did it, Mommy," Jeremy announced proudly as he held out the cup to her. "Hold it while I climb up."

Hannah took the cup, needing to blink back her tears. She couldn't imagine not trying to save her son's leg. Before she could do much more, she saw her son scramble up into Mark's lap and then hold out a hand to her, asking for his cup.

She could only smile at Jeremy and hand him the water.

It no longer seemed so important whether her son preferred her or Mark. She would share Jeremy with anyone who loved him as long as God saw fit to let her son have a healthy leg so he could run and play like other children.

"Please, Father," she whispered aloud.

Mark caught her gaze.

"Amen," he added to her prayer.

Just then a nurse stepped into the waiting room, a clipboard in her hand, and called, "Jeremy Nelson."

Hannah was sitting close enough to Mark that she could feel the jolt that went through him.

"He's a Nelson?" Mark asked in wonder. "I always assumed you used Stelling for him. I guess I should have asked. Not that anyone ever wanted to talk to me about Jeremy."

"I thought you knew," she said. "I listed you on the birth certificate and I thought—well, I guess I thought at that point that you'd come out of the coma in a few months."

"I'm here now," Mark said. If she wasn't mistaken, a tear was trailing down his cheek.

"Jeremy—" The nurse began her call again, so Hannah stood up.

"Here," she said and then cleared her throat so her voice was strong enough to reach the nurse. "We're here."

The three of them walked forward with Jeremy in the middle. She noticed that her son hadn't relinquished his plastic bag that carried his comic books. He had the handle looped over his arm, the bright colors of the heroes showing in the opening.

They had to separate in order to fit into the doctor's examination room, and Mark gestured for Hannah to go first as he stood behind Jeremy. She was glad he'd thought to keep their son between them. Jeremy might not be crying, but she knew he didn't want to be seen by a doctor. He'd appreciate being defended on all sides.

"There's no shots today," she turned to whisper to Jeremy so he wouldn't worry about that at least.

The doctor was sitting beside the exam table and smiling. "A big boy like you has probably already had his shots for school anyway."

The doctor was looking at Jeremy, but Hannah answered. "We did them last year. For day care."

It was while getting those shots the first time that she'd mentioned to her last doctor Jeremy seemed to be tired a lot. She'd wondered at the time if he was not getting enough sleep, and after the doctor gave him a brief exam, he said she was probably right.

There was only one visitor's chair in the room, so Mark suggested she take it. When she sank down into it, he stood behind her and put his hands on her shoulders. She was grateful for his presence. They both watched as Jeremy took off his shirt and climbed onto the exam table like the doctor told him to do.

Before doing anything, the doctor looked at Mark.

"Mr. Nelson?" he asked.

Mark nodded.

The doctor made a notation on a chart he had open on the counter behind him and then focused on Jeremy.

Hannah knew that chart already had the blood tests and X-rays from Jeremy's previous medical encounters, but the doctor was methodical about poking and prodding his patient anyway.

It seemed like it took hours, but Hannah looked at the clock and only ten minutes passed when the doctor seemed to be finished with the physical exam. He lifted Jeremy down from the table.

"You're a good boy," the doctor said as he patted Jeremy on the head.

Hannah would have preferred the doctor declare him a healthy boy, but she knew that wasn't likely given the concerned expression on the man's face.

"I'll need some more lab work," the doctor said and handed her a form. "You can stop at this place on the way out of town. I'll notify them when you leave here and they'll set it up for you so it'll be quick. Then we can go further."

Hannah nodded. Mark said he'd like to talk to the doctor a bit more, so Hannah put her hand around Jeremy's shoulder and started leading him back to the waiting room. She didn't blame Mark for needing to hear about the cost from the doctor. She would have wanted to verify that, as well.

*Oh, Lord*, she prayed silently without even thinking. *I can't do this without your help.*

She'd long ago decided that Jeremy was a gift from God. He kept her sane when she had no one else. The constant needs of a baby could distract almost anyone from their grief.

The prayers at least helped her gather her breath. Once in the waiting room with Jeremy, she sat down to wait for Mark. A doctor's time was valuable, so she didn't think Mark would be long.

It couldn't have been more than five minutes when he stepped back into the room. He wasn't smiling as he walked over to where she and Jeremy sat. Mark sank down in a chair beside Hannah and leaned closer to her ear.

"It's thirty thousand, all right," Mark whispered. "Payable on Monday morning."

"This coming Monday morning?" she asked, aghast. "That's so soon."

Mark nodded.

Well, she thought, more time wouldn't make much difference. "I'm already praying."

"For this kind of money, we need the church praying," Mark said as he stood up.

"I don't like to—" Hannah started to say she didn't like to broadcast her failings as a parent. But she had no choice in this. She'd tell the world she needed money if it would help.

She stood, too. "I'll ask Mrs. Hargrove to put it on the prayer chain myself."

There were few times when her pride didn't matter one iota, and all of them related to Jeremy. She doubted anyone thought she had thirty thousand dollars anyway.

Mark guided them out of the building and, within minutes, they were at the lab. That didn't take long and then they were driving back to Dry Creek with Jeremy asleep in his car seat.

"We didn't get ice cream," Mark said softly. They were already miles away from Billings.

"We've got some at the café," Hannah said. "I can get him a scoop of vanilla. They keep it for the folks who like their pie à la mode."

"Sounds good," Mark said.

They were both exhausted and remained silent for many miles.

"It's times like this when you bring out the family jewelry," Mark finally said, ruefully. "If I'd had any sense, I'd have given you a big fancy engagement ring in high school that you could sell. I had money then."

Hannah smiled. "You did give me that cereal box ring once."

Mark grunted. "If you still had it, we could find a buyer, I'm sure."

"I do have it, so there!" Hannah remembered when he gave her that ring and the kiss that followed.

Mark looked at her in astonishment. "Wasn't it a mood ring or something like that?"

"It was a love ring," she corrected him. "It was supposed to shine red when you thought about your beloved."

"And did it?" he asked.

She shook her head. "Just once." She paused. "The night we had our big fight."

Mark was silent a minute. Then he sighed. "I was such a fool that night."

"I suppose all kids make mistakes," she said.

"You didn't," he shot back. "You never went out drinking at all. Not once."

"Well, no," she admitted. "I didn't make *that* mistake. And you never did, either, until that night."

Mark nodded.

They rode in silence for a while, but Hannah felt better just having him sit next to her. She knew she should trust God to help them with Jeremy's treatment, but giving everything over to God was much easier said than done. It helped to have Mark there, as well.

She glanced back to see if Jeremy was still sleeping. He was and soundly.

"Do you think God will answer our prayers for the money we need?" she asked Mark.

He hesitated. "He said in the Bible He would meet all our needs."

"I know what the Bible says," Hannah replied. "I want to know what you think."

Mark glanced over and she knew she'd caught him.

"I sure hope so," he said. "But I remember—"

He didn't finish his sentence, but she knew.

"When our mothers each died," she said the words for him. They had prayed and mourned for their mothers in turn. It had been his mother first and then her adoptive mom.

"Well," she said and then stopped. There was nothing to be said, really. They both knew of times when people prayed and nothing seemed to happen. She supposed that was what trust was all about, though. Trusting that God would do the best thing even if you didn't agree with what that was.

From then on, she leaned back in the seat and watched the fields go by. Her father would have enjoyed seeing the crops, some recently harvested and others still growing. She always enjoyed the sway of the seasons here, the ebb and flow of crops. The greening and the browning of the grasses. Nothing stayed the same. It reminded her of God's grace in some ways. It was in His control—she didn't doubt that. It's just that she didn't know if He'd be planting or pruning when it came to her.

## Chapter Ten

Mark sat at the table in his family home the next morning. His sister, Allie, had come over to fix his father some breakfast even though she and her new husband, Clay West, had their new home almost finished. Located to the right of the main ranch house, it was a sleek structure of rock and natural wood. Mark liked to have his sister walking around in their old home, though, and he was glad she'd come this morning.

"I'm thinking of going to see Mr. Gaines at the bank and asking for a loan," he said softly as his father sipped his coffee and his sister buttered a piece of nicely browned toast.

"What?" the two of them said in near unison. He could see the shock on their faces.

"I need thirty thousand dollars," Mark explained. "And Mr. Gaines always cheered me on at football games and even came to see me ride in the rodeo."

"He was a fan, all right," his father said slowly. "But thirty thousand is a lot of money. You know he'll never take the ranch as collateral since it's already put up for the money we borrowed a year ago to—"

Mark appreciated his father's reluctance to cite the bill, but it wasn't a secret to anyone. "I know what you did to pay my costs at the nursing home, but I need a loan. I have nothing else. Well, there is my pickup, but it won't bring in more than a couple of thousand. And I suppose I could sell my rodeo trophies and get a few hundred."

"You've been giving this some thought," his father said. "Does this mean you're considering leaving us?"

"No," Mark said, surprised at the look of worry on his father's face. "What makes you say that?"

"What else would you need that much money for?" the other man answered.

Mark could see he wouldn't escape the conversation without telling them everything, and really there was no need to keep his family in the dark.

"Jeremy has some special kind of leukemia and he needs a new medical treatment," Mark said. "Hannah and I took him to the doctor yesterday and—" He spread his hands. He'd never felt more helpless. "Without the treatment, the boy will likely lose his right leg."

Mark couldn't bear to mention that his son might even die.

"Oh!" Their cries of distress came together.

"I can't let that happen," Mark said.

"Of course not," his sister said, and his father nodded emphatically. Mark knew they both loved the boy.

"Hannah and I have talked," Mark continued. "We feel we need to provide our son with the best care we can—Jeremy deserves that. So I'm going to be asking Mr. Gaines to loan me part of the money, at least."

And then the questions started. Mark could only pull

out the flyer that the doctor had given him after Hannah and Jeremy left the office yesterday.

"This explains it," Mark said.

He let them both read the fact sheet for a few minutes before he made his announcement. "I told the doctor I'd have the money for him by Monday morning. He said there's a window of opportunity to do the procedure and the soonest he can do the work is Wednesday. He said he'd put the order in for what he needs late Monday so it will get to him in time."

"But what happens if you don't have the money?" his father asked.

"Then the doctor won't do the stem cell treatment," Mark said. "He'll start the standard procedure instead. That goes on for a while."

"Is there something wrong with that?" Allie asked. "Just going with the usual thing."

"Ninety-five percent of the time the standard treatment ends with amputation," Mark said. "This is a special rare kind of cancer and the chemo doesn't seem to stop it in most cases."

Allie gasped. "No."

"They'll try chemo and radiation, of course, but if they don't work—and as I said, likely it won't—the situation gets worse, and then sometimes even amputation isn't enough."

"Then what happens?" Allie asked.

"He—" Mark still couldn't say the words, but he could see Allie figuring it out.

"No," she shook her head. "He can't die. He's too young."

"Young children die all the time," Mark said.

Everyone was speechless and then Allie started.

"We have about three thousand dollars in the ranch account," she said. "Three hundred in our Christmas account. And Clay and I could kick in our furniture money. That's all we haven't spent. It's about two thousand and you're welcome to it. We can get along without a new sofa. We might be able to sell one of the colts, but we won't have the money by Monday."

"I've got a bit saved from my Social Security checks," his father said. "Not much, but it's yours."

Mark was touched. "That will all help. If Mr. Gaines can see his way to lending me twenty thousand dollars, I think we could piece it all together."

"Well," his father said, "the man has always seemed to like you."

"But is that enough?" Allie asked.

"I'll wear one of my rodeo belt buckles to remind him that I'm a winner," Mark said. Then he stilled the voice inside that said he had been a winner, but he wasn't currently one. That part needed to change. He must be a hero for Hannah's sake and for Jeremy's sake and, Mark admitted, for his own self-respect. He just didn't know how to do it.

"Letting him see one of those belt buckles on you might work," his father said cautiously. "A man like him knows what they represent."

"It has to work," Mark agreed.

Just then the door opened and the wrangler, Randy, stepped inside.

"Eating without me?" Randy said. His voice was jovial until he looked around more closely. "What's wrong? I was only teasing. I already had breakfast."

"It's Jeremy," Allie said, almost crying. Randy knew

the boy from his visits to the ranch. "He needs an opera-tion to save his leg and we don't have the money for it."

"Well, money shouldn't stop anybody," the ranch hand declared indignantly.

"I'm afraid in this case it does," Mark said. "It's a new procedure and the insurance won't cover it because it's not routine. And we need thirty thousand dollars."

Randy whistled. "That's not cheap."

"No," Mark said.

They were all silent for a while.

"It'll be on the prayer chain later today," Mark added. "Maybe with everyone praying, we'll make it."

No one looked confident of that, so he reminded them, "Look what prayer did for me. Everyone said there was no hope for me when I was in that coma and the church here just kept praying."

Just recalling Mark's recovery made them all brighten up and nod. They started to eat again and, be-fore long, breakfast was over and Mark was ready to go into Dry Creek. He wanted to talk to Mrs. Hargrove. She had organized the prayers for him. He'd ask her to pray for his meeting with Mr. Gaines.

"Here." Allie handed Mark a bunch of papers. "Some mail for you."

Mark took the letters and flyers almost without thinking. He was hoping Mrs. Hargrove would have some encouraging words and suggestions for him about how to get people to pray effectively. He was out the door when he noticed that the sheet of paper on top of the pile was a call for contestants in a rodeo com-ing up soon in northern Montana. This Saturday after-noon, in fact.

Mark felt a burst of excitement before he realized

a rodeo did him no good. It was, however, exactly the kind of thing he had turned to when he needed money before his coma. He's sign up to ride in one of the events and come back a hero with enough of what he needed to solve the problems of the day. He'd done that once when the pep band needed new uniforms. He'd always remember walking down the length of the gym that morning with the band playing and everyone in the athletic department cheering as he waved the prize check in the air.

Those days were gone. The doctors said he would likely die if he ever fell from a horse again. He couldn't resist reading down the list of competitions, though, wondering if there wasn't some event that would be safe enough. There was nothing. Even the clown work was dangerous.

Mark put the stack of mail on the floorboard of his pickup and went to the tack room. He wouldn't get much applause, but he could still be a hero with his handyman tools. He was determined to find another lock and key combination. This morning as Mr. Stelling ranted about being awoken, Mark had learned that the main house on their ranch didn't have a working key, either. If he was going to keep Hannah and Jeremy safe, he might as well keep the old man secure, too. That's what a family did. Mark was surprised at how happy the thought made him. He wondered when Hannah was going to tell Jeremy who his father was. It seemed a boy facing trouble would want to know he had someone else on his side.

Hannah was tired the next morning. She slept in a little while and didn't get out of bed until half past six o'clock. That meant she didn't have time to fix Jeremy the kind of egg breakfast she felt he needed. She looked over in the bed and saw he was curled into a ball, still sleeping. He'd refused to go to bed without his handful of comic books, and one of them was still clenched in his fist. She wondered if she should tell him he had to leave the superhero comics on the floor beside the bed when he was going to sleep. She gave a sigh just thinking about it. She didn't have the heart to refuse him anything. Not with things the way they were.

"Sweetie," she whispered as she lightly shook Jeremy's shoulder. "Time to get up."

She got no response so she shook again. Just when she was getting worried, Jeremy groaned and rolled over.

"Stay here?" he asked, his voice slurred with sleep. He hadn't even opened his eyes.

"You can't," Hannah whispered back. "Mommy needs to go to work today and you can't stay alone."

"Callie's here," her son said as though that solved the problem. The furry calico cat was stretching on the floor on Jeremy's side of the bed.

"You know a cat isn't a good babysitter," Hannah said, a smile in her voice. She knew how fond her son was of that cat. "But I'll tell Mrs. Hargrove that you want to nap for a while even though it's morning."

The older woman would understand. Hannah had stopped by Mrs. Hargrove's house last night and told her everything. She wouldn't be surprised Jeremy would want to rest more.

"Okay," her son said wearily as he sat up in bed.

Hannah's heart broke a little. He tried his very best to be good. He didn't deserve the troubles he was facing. Several times when they were getting ready for bed last night, she had started to talk to Jeremy about any fears or concerns he had about the illness. He wouldn't even look at her; instead, he kept mouthing the words he could read in those comic books of his. She finally decided the conversation could wait until later today when they were both rested.

Hannah took a quick shower first and then dressed herself and Jeremy. She'd given him a bath last night in the hope it would relax him. This morning all he had to do was use a washcloth on his face and brush his teeth.

For herself, Hannah was grateful for the informal outfit the waitresses wore at the café. She had another pair of clean jeans and a second red T-shirt. She wrapped a rubber band around her hair and pulled it back into a ponytail. She was strapping Jeremy into his car seat when she noticed his hair hadn't been brushed.

"Here we go," she said as she spread her fingers and swiped at his hair. It looked pretty good except for the cowlick behind his ear. Of course, that sometimes didn't get tamed even with a vigorous brushing from a real comb.

She ended by dropping a kiss on his forehead and hurrying around to get behind the wheel. She saw her father walking out of his house when she went by but she didn't take time to stop and chat. She planned to invite Mrs. Hargrove to bring herself and Jeremy over to the café for breakfast, but she needed to hurry to be on time for work.

The next hour was a whirlwind. The strange thing was that the faster Hannah poured coffee and brought out platters of food from the kitchen, the calmer she felt about life. Ever since she had arranged with Mrs. Hargrove last night to put a request on the prayer chain about Jeremy's illness and the treatment he needed, her mind had been churning, trying to find a source for the money they required.

The breakfast rush was slowing down when Mrs. Hargrove brought Jeremy to the door. A couple of local ranch hands, Randy from the Nelson ranch among them, were the only ones left. They were sitting at a table in the middle of the room, drinking a last cup of coffee. She'd already removed their plates and refreshed their beverages. Lois was clearing the dishes from an empty table and she looked up, along with Hannah, when Mrs. Hargrove and Jeremy walked in.

Lois stopped what she was doing and watched Jeremy climb into a chair at the closest table to the door. He had his usual fistful of comic books in one hand and he carefully spread them out in front of him.

"He's such a brave boy," she whispered to Hannah, who had told her coworker about the leukemia before they started their shifts.

Lois looked ready to cry, but Hannah figured her son wouldn't like to have people weeping over him.

"That's because he's a cowboy," Hannah said loud enough for the boy to hear. She could see from where she stood that he had his Davy Crockett comic on top of his pile.

Jeremy beamed at her words and picked up a fork, standing it upright in his fist.

The ranch hands heard her statement, too, and turned to look at the boy, kind expressions on their faces.

"We've got a horse out at your Grandpa Nelson's ranch just waiting for a youngster like you to take a ride," Randy said, his good cheer filling the room.

Hannah knew that Randy had been at the Nelson

ranch a few times when Jeremy had visited. She nodded to the wrangler in thanks.

"You'll want to eat up and get strong," one of the other men said in a hearty voice. "Drink some juice with breakfast."

"I can't get strong," Jeremy replied, his voice full of regret and sadness. "I have to go to the doctor."

Everyone was silent.

"I don't like doctors," Jeremy said with finality. "They put you to sleep and you don't wake up."

Except for Randy, the other men were all looking at Hannah with bewildered expressions on their faces. She didn't know what to say. No one had said anything like that yesterday.

She stepped closer to her son and squatted down until she was level with his eyes. "Everyone just wants to help you. But you don't have to worry about not waking up. You get up every morning and then you have breakfast."

Jeremy gave an uncertain nod, but Lois had taken a more direct answer to his feelings.

"How about some grape juice?" she said to Jeremy as she handed the boy one of the cups the café used for coffee.

"That's a cup for a big guy," Jeremy said, excited, as he reached for the thick white mug. He stopped short of curling his fingers around the handle. "Is it okay, Mommy?"

Hannah nodded, blinking her own tears back.

While Jeremy blissfully took a big gulp of his juice, Hannah noticed he had a purple mustache above his lip, but she didn't say anything. Lois brought a cup of coffee for Mrs. Hargrove, too.

Hannah stepped over and then bent down to give the

older woman a hug. "Thank you for bringing Jeremy over." She straightened. "Did he manage to sleep any more after I dropped him off?"

Mrs. Hargrove nodded. "He slept for about an hour."

"I'll bring you both something to eat," Hannah said as she pulled out her order pad. "I know Jeremy likes a scrambled egg and toast." She looked at Mrs. Hargrove. "How about you?"

"Some toast would go well with my coffee," the older woman answered. "And maybe some of the strawberry preserves they have here. I can tell they are home-canned."

"A woman north of here makes a dozen pints each summer for the café," Hannah said as she put her order pad back into the pocket of her apron. "We buy extra strawberries for the chiffon pies, too."

As she turned to take the order into the kitchen, Hannah noticed that the three ranch hands had their heads together and were whispering fiercely. Lois had been there seconds ago, filling their coffee cups, and Hannah expected the other waitress was giving them the gist of the prayer request that was going to be public this morning. Or maybe Randy had already heard the facts from Mark. In any event, Mrs. Hargrove said she was going to start the telephone chain as soon as possible after Hannah dropped Jeremy off so the message was likely already reaching some people.

Hannah had to pass the trio on her way to the kitchen and she decided it was good practice for her to appear nonchalant. People were going to be talking. She had a pot of coffee in her hand and she would look natural here if nothing else.

Just then she heard the sounds of a pickup stopping

in front of the café. She recognized the purr of that engine and had to stop herself from waltzing by the small mirror near the kitchen and being sure her hair didn't look squashed in the hairnet she wore.

At least she had time to catch her balance before Mark opened the door and greeted everyone.

"Can I get you anything?" Hannah asked as Mark walked over to the table where Jeremy and Mrs. Hargrove were situated.

"Come sit with us," Mark suggested as he pulled out one of the chairs for himself and then reached for another.

The morning light did not fill the inside of the café like it did some days. Instead, there were shadows everywhere. Mark's eyes went from hazel to black depending on the angle of his face as he sat down and looked at her. He wore a slight smile and it drew her to him.

"I was thinking more along the lines of a cup of coffee," Hannah said as she walked closer to the table.

"That, too," Mark answered, his smile deepening. He was happy.

Suddenly she understood. "You've thought of some way to get that money, haven't you?"

She sat in the chair Mark had pulled out for her.

"I have hopes, but nothing concrete," Mark whispered as he scooted his chair closer to her.

Hannah didn't even bother to tamp down her relief. If Mark had an idea, it would work. "What is it?"

Mark didn't answer and Hannah noticed out the corner of her eye that Jeremy was squirming in his chair. Mrs. Hargrove was watching them all serenely.

"Let me guess," Jeremy finally called out.

Hannah turned to her son in astonishment. The boy's cheeks were pink with excitement. He was waving his thin arms as fast as he could and he was looking back and forth from Hannah to Mark like he couldn't wait to see who would answer first.

"Go ahead and guess," Mark said as he looked down at Jeremy.

Hannah's breath caught, taken back by the shining affection she saw on Mark's face as he studied her son—well, their son, she thought. She had not expected this. She knew Mark wanted Jeremy to know he was his father. But she figured Mark was concerned about the legality of things. He'd always been orderly. And he would want to cheer at sporting events and brag about his son. She didn't begrudge him any of that. But she hadn't expected Mark to love Jeremy as much as it looked like he did.

She suddenly realized she needed to tell Jeremy who Mark was and she needed to do it soon. It wasn't fair to either of them to keep putting it off. Maybe after Jeremy finished his guessing, she would find a way to tell him.

Of course, she reminded herself as she studied Jeremy, he might not be too quick about guessing. She could see by the shine in his eyes that Jeremy liked having the whole café turned to him.

"The money will come from—" Jeremy paused for effect. Then he reached down and grabbed a comic. "Davy Crockett! King of the wild frontier!"

Mark grinned and winked at Hannah. "I'll have to track the mountain man down and ask him for help. He might have dug up some gold on one of his adventures."

Jeremy giggled with joy.

"Or maybe the masked man can get it from the bank robbers," Jeremy said as he held another comic up.

"Hmm," Mark pretended to consider Jeremy's suggestions. "I could try that, too."

Hannah sat there enthralled. She'd never expected Jeremy to be as captivated by anyone as he was with Mark. And then, to make the feeling sweeter, Mark reached over and took her hand so she was included in the warmth of the moment, too.

"It's fine to tell him," Hannah said as she leaned over closer to Mark. "Any time."

Mark nodded, the smile on his face deepening. "I'd like that."

Mrs. Hargrove sat forward with a smile on her face. Hannah figured the older woman knew a special moment was coming up.

Jeremy held up the final comic book. "This guy can fly. He can go up to the top of mountains and bring back some money."

Hannah enjoyed watching the imagination in her son.

"But can he bring back kisses?" Mark asked the boy as he leaned over and kissed the top of Jeremy's head.

Her son started to giggle and pointed at her. "Do Mommy, too."

"I—" Hannah tried to think of a coherent protest.

But Mark was too fast. He swooped over and kissed her on the cheek.

"Oh." Hannah was both relieved and very disappointed.

Before she could say anything more, though, Mark moved slightly and cocked an eyebrow at her.

"Shall we give him something to remember?" he whispered.

She could feel the blush crawl up her neck, but she couldn't seem to speak. Mark must have been encouraged by her lack of protest because the next thing she knew he kissed her, the way he used to do. His lips were gentle and he touched her cheek in a way that made her long for more. She knew she should pull away, but she seemed unable to do so.

Everyone was silent as she stared at Mark. She remembered how his eyes changed colors with his emotions. How his jaw flexed as he debated something. The warmth of his breath made her knees weak. If she hadn't been sitting down, she would have slid right to the floor.

"Now do Grandma," Jeremy commanded and Hannah realized where she was. That was the name Jeremy called Mrs. Hargrove. It seemed to suit them both.

"Now you're being silly," the older woman protested.

Hannah was surprised the woman wasn't looking at her and Mark in shock, but she didn't appear at all rattled by the kiss she'd just witnessed.

"He's only going to kiss your Mommy that way," Mrs. Hargrove added, leaning toward Jeremy and smoothing down his cowlick.

Hannah decided Mark must agree with her that Mrs. Hargrove was being kind because he stood up, took a step and kissed the older woman on her forehead.

"Oh," she said. "You didn't have to do that."

"It was my pleasure," Mark said as Mrs. Hargrove's face got pink.

"It might be different," he said. "But no less sincere." Then he bowed.

It took a minute for Jeremy to finish giggling.

"I didn't know you found yourself a grandma," Mark said when things quieted down.

Jeremy nodded and all traces of laughter were gone. "Grandmas make cookies for little boys. Chocolate chip ones. They're my favorites."

"That's very helpful," Mark said, matching her son's serious tone.

Hannah took a deep breath. She knew Mark was leading up to his announcement and she suddenly wanted everything to go perfectly for him and Jeremy. She might not be ready to trust anyone inside her heart right now, but she wanted Jeremy to have all the love in the world. She supposed mothers were made that way—they needed to be strong to protect their children, but they wanted the softness for their children that they dared not allow themselves to feel sometimes.

"Now that you have a grandmother and a mother," Mark said, trying so hard to sound casual that Hannah could tell he was nervous, "what would you think about having a father, too? Like me."

Hannah felt her stomach clench. Jeremy was sitting there, looking at Mark like he couldn't understand the question.

"I don't have a father," Jeremy said, his voice clear. "I have a mommy."

Hannah noticed then that her son was curling his fist around those comic books he'd brought with him.

"Most little boys have a mother and a father," Hannah said softly, thinking that perhaps Jeremy just needed permission to be enthused at the prospect. "Mark wants to be a good father."

But her son shook his head vehemently and climbed down from his chair. He had the same stubborn look on his face that she had seen on Mark's countless times as they were growing up in this town.

"I don't need a father," Jeremy said, facing the whole table. There was no trace of a smile on his face any longer. "I just need my mother."

The whole café was quiet and Hannah realized everyone there had been following the conversation. Not that there were many folks there. Lois and the three ranch hands had no doubt heard it all, but that was only four other people. Even as Hannah told herself that, she realized that everyone within miles would know this story before supper. People probably hadn't stopped gossiping about why she'd come back yet and everyone knew Mark was Jeremy's father. They were likely all waiting for some word on what was going to happen with the three of them.

Hannah looked over at Mark. She had never intended to embarrass him. It hadn't occurred to her that Jeremy wouldn't welcome a father in his life. He had seemed to like Mark. In fact, she would have guessed he liked Mark more than he did any other man he had met.

"Jeremy just needs some time," Mrs. Hargrove said softly as she stood to follow after the boy. Jeremy was already reaching for the door handle. The compassion was evident on the older woman's face.

"It's my fault," Hannah said as she watched her son leave the café with Mrs. Hargrove trailing behind him.

Mark looked over at her. "And just how is it your fault?"

His voice was stark and his question incredulous.

"He's taken his cues from me," Hannah whispered, realizing as she said it that it was true. She was afraid to trust anyone and her son had learned to live the same way she did. She was polite, but she never let anyone close. Not anymore.

"Oh, so you don't have any use for me, either," Mark said bitterly. "Is that what you're saying?"

"No," she protested. She didn't know how she'd gotten trapped in this moment. "You've been so helpful to me. You painted that ceiling for me and Jeremy. You brought us a bed. You went with us to the doctor's visit. You even did my father's harvesting."

Hannah knew she was leaving out some of Mark's kind acts, but he was looking at her like none of what he had done mattered.

"I'm so sorry," she finished. "He needs to think about this. I'll talk to him."

Some strong emotion flashed over Mark's face. "You can't force the boy to accept me."

Hannah looked around her, seeking an answer from somewhere. That's when she noticed the others in the café must have tiptoed out the back door in the kitchen, because she and Mark were alone in the main part of the restaurant.

"He just doesn't know what a father is," Hannah said, pleading for extra time for them both. "He hasn't had a father."

The emotions seemed to have left Mark.

"He's always had me," Mark said softly as he stood up. "And so have you. I might not have been here to help you, but in my heart I have always cared about you."

The words warmed Hannah until she realized the sound of defeat that lingered after he'd finished speaking them.

"I appreciate that," she said as she forced back her tears. She meant to say more, but she paused because she didn't know what exactly she wanted to convey to Mark.

He looked at her a moment and then turned, his

shoulders slumped. She impulsively rose to go after him, but she didn't follow through. Before she knew it, he was gone.

The café grew cold as she stood there. She realized she had just received what she wanted. She didn't need to worry about being left by Mark because she'd left him. She was standing strong and not relying on anyone, but that meant she didn't have anyone beside her, either.

She listened to the sounds of Mark's pickup backing away from the café. Finally, she heard the door to the kitchen open. Hannah turned and saw Lois coming toward her with a tray.

"I thought you'd like a cup of hot tea," Lois said. "It always settles my nerves."

"Thank you," Hannah whispered as she walked over to a different table and sat down. She'd probably never sit at the table by the door again. If she did, she'd find herself remembering the cracks in her heart that had happened as she sat there.

The tea was spiced and had extra lemon in it. As the sweet flavor comforted her, Hannah watched Lois walk around the café, serving coffee to a rancher who came in every week or so for some of Lois's chiffon pie.

"Are you ever lonely?" Hannah asked Lois when the other waitress came over to ask if she wanted more tea.

Lois nodded. "I'd give anything to have a good man care about me."

Hannah looked up at that. "But you have guys flocking in here every day to get a piece of your chiffon pie."

Lois shrugged. "Oh, most of them would take me out. Of course, the one I want to ask me out doesn't, but the others—they just want a good time. And me, I want a home with someone who is in it for thick and thin. Someone who will stand beside me in the hard times. You know what I mean?"

Hannah nodded. She did know.

Lois went off to take more coffee to the rancher finishing his breakfast.

The thing with a cracked heart, Hannah told herself as she finished her tea, was that it did not stop one's life from going forward. She still had to worry about getting the money for Jeremy's procedure. She still had to go home tonight and coax her son into talking about why he wasn't opening his arms to the man who was his father. And, she told herself as the café door opened again, she still had to help Lois serve the people who stopped here to eat.

It was going to be a long day, she thought as she stood up.

## *Chapter Eleven*

Mark gripped the steering wheel as he drove down the freeway toward Miles City. Everything was going wrong. Before leaving the café, he had left the door open on his pickup for a few minutes while he checked the tire on the passenger side. He hadn't noticed until he was more than halfway to his destination that he had a stowaway passenger huddled under an open newspaper on the floor of the cab—the sneaky cat that Jeremy called his Callie. Apparently, she could be quiet when it suited her.

Mark rolled his eyes. "What am I supposed to do with you?" he asked the feline.

She smugly ignored him and licked her paw. Mark figured that driving off with Jeremy's cat involved some treachery on the part of that feisty animal. Mark was too big to fight fairly and the cat knew it. But this escapade would not endear Mark to his son; Jeremy would likely protect his pet with his life. No one would believe the cat had gotten into his pickup voluntarily since she never left Jeremy's side and didn't seem overly fond of Mark. It was bad enough that he wasn't a comic book hero, Mark figured. He didn't need to be a villain in a cat abduction story. Even Hannah would join forces with their son in condemnation of him.

Just thinking about Hannah almost made Mark turn around right away, but he realized he was already more than halfway to Miles City. He could call Mrs. Hargrove when he got to the bank and explain what happened quicker than he could let anyone know if he turned around now and retraced his route.

Empty wheat fields lined the road to Miles City. Mark saw a rabbit or two bounding along near the fences. He liked this time of year when the harvesting was done. The pickup hit a bump in the road and the cat hissed and then settled down to glare at Mark.

"I guess you probably thought it would all go smoother," Mark said, agreeing with that sentiment. "Well, welcome to the club."

By this time, Callie had swatted the newspaper aside and was standing on top of the stack of papers that had been lying on the floor. She had already wrinkled the rodeo flyer and was standing on the envelopes as she looked around.

"I know you smelled the sandwich," Mark said to the cat. "But I already brought it up by me."

Mark had made a tuna sandwich and tucked it into a thin cool pack so he could take it with him when he left the house this morning. It was noon now, but he wasn't stopping.

"I couldn't eat a thing," Mark said conversationally to his reluctant companion. "Not hungry."

Mark couldn't remember what he'd eaten earlier, but he supposed it was scrambled eggs and toast. It's what he usually ate when breakfasting in his father's house.

"I suppose you want something to eat though," Mark added after a few minutes.

The cat meowed, and Mark thought he detected a bit of a prima donna attitude in the beast.

"Well, you'll have to wait," Mark said in case the cat was planning to claw its way into the cool pack that was on the dashboard in front of Mark. An easy snap was all that kept the cat out of the pack as it was. Callie did look at him hopefully, though.

"If I open up that sandwich, the whole pickup will smell of tuna and I'm not going into that bank stinking like pickled fish," Mark said.

Not that using a gimmick of some kind was a bad idea, he thought. He'd heard of one man who had gotten a loan because he could twirl four plates in the air at one time.

Mark's only claim to fame was those years lost in a coma. People were sure interested in what that was like. Most bankers wouldn't consider it an asset for a loan, though.

"Mr. Gaines watched me play sports all through high school," Mark reminded himself with a sideways glance at the cat. "And he watched me do some riding in the rodeo. I'm counting on his remembering me. He'll know that I don't quit. That I've always ridden any horse I draw. That I struggle and fight to win. He should know I'll be good for any money that I can borrow, don't you think?"

The cat was dozing by then so Mark was left with his thoughts. Which didn't please him. When he finished fretting about the loan, the hurt of this morning kept pressing closer to him. It was his fault, really, that Jeremy had rejected him. A man with any sense should have slowly worked up to the announcement with Jeremy instead of being so abrupt. It's just that he'd enjoyed his interactions with the boy and had assumed that his son would be pleased to know that he was his father.

And that wasn't even the worst of it, Mark admitted to himself. It wasn't just the boy; he wanted the whole family—Jeremy, Hannah and even the old man. Mark felt he belonged with them even if he and Hannah had not said their vows. Well, and at this point, might never say them if he read Hannah right.

He should have planned better, he told himself. He was so used to winning easily that he'd never learned to work for success. He wondered if it was too late to launch a campaign for the heart of his new family.

He thought hard for a few minutes. "That's the problem right there," he said aloud. "I don't have anything anymore to give them."

His family's farm was broke. They'd make their way back to being comfortable eventually, but it would take some years, and a woman might not want to wait that long.

"I should have asked her to marry me in high school," he said finally. "I was a winner back then."

Mark made the mistake of glancing down at that wayward cat and was irritated at the triumphant look in the feline's eyes. "You think it's easy to charm a woman, do you? Well, you should try it some time. The only reason Hannah accepts you is because you're Jeremy's cat."

Mark knew Hannah wasn't so shallow that she was only interested in the prizes a man could win, but it would certainly make him feel better to know he'd accomplished something to at least get her attention.

The town of Miles City appeared before he expected it and the bank stood where it always had square in the middle of the business area, a two-story brick building with big windows. He'd felt awestruck as a boy when he visited the place with his father. There was always a strip of green mown grass around the bank and a row of colorful flowers around the edge of the building.

After Mark stepped down from his pickup, he wished he'd thought to bring a present of some kind so he'd be able to give something to the banker. He couldn't give money, of course. That would be a bribe. And it was too late to bring one of the pies from the café.

He looked around the cab of his pickup as though something would appear suddenly. Finally he moved and the sunlight shone on his belt buckle, reflecting a flash of light on the steering wheel.

"Of course, I remember what I was going to do," Mark said, not speaking to the cat this time even though she lifted her head. He unclipped the buckle and saw reflected light swirl everywhere. Holding the buckle in his hand, he mused. He had been fortunate to win six of these prized buckles, but the one he held was the most expensive and his favorite. The rodeo association plated their first-place buckles with real silver and quality brass, but they'd added a few Montana opals to this one. It was the last buckle he'd won and he was especially proud of it because it was for bull riding. He slipped the buckle into the pocket of his jacket.

Mr. Gaines was in his office and, judging from the twinkling black eyes peering out through his horn-rimmed glasses, the older man appeared delighted to see Mark. He didn't look as thrilled to see the cat walk in behind Mark, but he didn't say anything.

Instead, he leaned forward to Mark with his hand outstretched. "You're looking good. I can't believe you're here. My son idolizes you—well, he used to when you played football. You were a real cowboy when you rode those broncs, too."

Mark felt his nerves relax. He had this. He shook hands with the man and they both sat down in the expensively upholstered chairs in the bank's corner office. Mark didn't care for the look in Callie's eyes as she reached out a paw toward one of the chairs, so he bent down and picked her up.

"Coffee?" Mr. Gaines offered.

"Thanks, but no," Mark said as he settled the unwilling cat onto his lap.

"I hear Dry Creek has a few good football players this fall," Mr. Gaines said, his voice cordial. The town of Dry Creek didn't have its own school, but they did have enough town spirit to form a cheering squad for the local kids who went to a bigger town for school.

"We always have one or two," Mark agreed. "It's all the farmwork that does it. Gives us all shoulder muscles and strong backs."

"I prefer the rodeos myself," Mr. Gaines said. "But I watch athletics, too. To support the community."

"You do your part, that's for sure," Mark said.

Mr. Gaines nodded. "So, what can I help you with today?"

Mark had practiced the words in his mind, but what came out was, "I need a loan."

"Oh," Mr. Gaines said, his eyebrow rising slightly.

"You've watched me play sports," Mark said. That was one point he remembered he was going to make. "I fight to win and I would pay every penny of a loan back, with interest. If I needed to, I could ride the rodeo circuit until I paid you back."

Everything was silent for a few minutes.

"I thought you couldn't ride rodeo anymore," the banker said slowly. "I heard the doctors didn't recommend it."

"Oh, doctors," Mark said with a wave of his free hand. "They don't recommend walking across the street. They're all afraid of lawsuits."

The banker didn't say anything, but he appeared to be thinking.

"It might not be bull riding or broncs or anything," Mark said eagerly. "But I could do something."

"Is this for business?" Mr. Gaines finally asked. "I usually talk with your father about any ranch loans in the spring."

Mark shook his head. "My son needs a medical procedure done."

Mark didn't feel like revealing anything more about Jeremy's condition. His son was not the one under the microscope. It was Mark.

"Ah," Mr. Gaines murmured. "Is this Hannah's—?"

The banker's voice trailed off and Mark only nodded.

Then he remembered the rodeo belt buckle he had brought. He reached into his jacket pocket and pulled out the buckle before holding it out to the banker. A brass bull almost jumped off the metalwork. "I won this by riding that big Brahma bull for three minutes and forty-two seconds in that rodeo they have every year up by Havre. I just got a flyer about the one they're getting ready for on Saturday afternoon. You going?"

"I usually do," the banker said.

"Me, too," Mark said and then held the buckle closer to the other man. "Thought you might like to have this. Sort of a souvenir of all the times you cheered me on."

"I did see some fine rides," Mr. Gaines said with a smile. "You were really something. But you should keep that buckle. You won it."

"I wouldn't mind parting with it if it meant a loan," Mark said, surprised that it was true.

Mr. Gaines stopped smiling and studied him. "How much do you need, son?"

"Thirty thousand," Mark said and he saw the other man frown slightly. "But I'd settle for twenty-five. I can maybe sell my pickup and borrow some from my family. Even twenty might do."

"That's a bit steep for unsecured loans," Mr. Gaines said. "Or do you have something for collateral?"

Mark shook his head. "Not for that amount."

"Well," Mr. Gaines said, "I can bring it to the board on Friday evening. You certainly are a well-known member of this community and we try to support our own when we can."

Mark let out the breath he'd been holding. "So, there's a chance?"

"A small one," Mr. Gaines said as he stood. "We don't generally make our calls until the Monday after the meeting, but I can call you Saturday morning before I head out to the rodeo and give you a heads-up. You can fill out the forms next week."

Mark nodded. He had a chance. "Call me at the café in Dry Creek. I'll wait there for word."

Mark wanted to be close to Hannah when he heard about the loan.

"I'll do that," the banker said.

Mark put the buckle back in his pocket and shook hands again with Mr. Gaines. Then Mark tucked the cat under his arm and walked out of the banker's office.

Mark knew the teller and asked to use the phone to call Mrs. Hargrove. He was given permission and kept his remarks brief. Jeremy apparently had been napping and hadn't noticed that Callie was even missing.

The sun was so strong outside that, when Mark stepped outside the bank, it made him stop and squint. When he opened the door of his pickup, the air inside was hotter than he expected even though he'd parked in the shade of the building.

Mark set the cat on the passenger seat and then climbed inside himself. It was time to go home. He'd no more had that thought when he realized he could no longer pinpoint exactly where his home was. He lived with his father on his family's ranch, but his heart was with Hannah and Jeremy.

This was a bitter realization because as far as Mark could see, he had one chance to win the affections of the woman and boy: he had to get his hands on the thirty thousand dollars for that procedure. If there was ever a need for him to be a hero, the time was now. The cat jumped from the seat to the floorboard of his pickup and landed on the stack of mail. The rodeo flyer was still at the top of the pile.

"Don't tear that," Mark said softly as he reached down and pulled the sheet of paper away from the cat's claws. He laid the flyer against the center of the steering wheel and smoothed it out before letting his eyes scan the listing of competitions one more time.

"There's got to be something I can do to get some prize money," he muttered to himself as he studied the list carefully. He needed a backup plan in case he didn't get the loan.

\* \* \*

Twenty miles away, Hannah and Lois were sitting at the small table in the kitchen of the Dry Creek café, taking a break. It was two o'clock and they'd served the last of the lunch crowd. The dining area was empty and they would hear any customer who might enter. They each had a cup of tea in front of them. In addition, Lois had a long piece of paper and a pencil in her hand.

"If we get all of the supplies tomorrow," Lois said as she added to the list she had going, "we can bake the pies on Friday and have them ready for the sale on Saturday morning before the rodeo. People will be driving through. We might need to offer to keep them in the big refrigerator until they drive back through after the rodeo, but we can do that."

"You're sure you're willing to do all this work?" Hannah asked for the third time since they'd sat down for the planning. She still couldn't believe anyone would go to so much effort to help her and Jeremy. Lois had known them for only a few days. Hannah couldn't wait to tell Mark about the plan.

"I won't be doing it alone," Lois said as she looked up with a smile.

"I'm willing to do everything I can," Hannah said fervently. "But I've never baked a pie before."

"There's a first time for everything," Lois said cheerfully. "You'll do fine. And, you'll see, there will be others coming to help, too. You're a hometown girl and Dry Creek folks take care of their own."

"Oh," Hannah said. Lois hadn't lived here more than a year so she didn't know about Hannah's past. "I didn't grow up here. I've always been an outsider."

"What's that supposed to mean?" Lois said with a frown.

"These kinds of things were always done for the kids who grew up here," Hannah said. "Not for me. I was adopted."

Lois was silent and Hannah didn't have the courage to look at the other woman to see what she was thinking.

"It was fine, though," Hannah added. "I was grateful for what I had at the Stellings'. At least, when my mom was alive."

"Sounds like it was a hard time," Lois said sympathetically and Hannah looked up and nodded.

Hannah didn't want the other woman to give up on the pie bake sale she was planning, but Hannah felt she should know the score.

"Well, Randy Collins said it would work," Lois said. "And I think he knows what he's talking about."

The idea to have a chiffon pie bake sale had come a few hours ago from the ranch hands who had been having breakfast in the café earlier. It had been Randy's idea, but all three of them promised to spread the word of the sale around the countryside, especially after Lois estimated she and Hannah could bake two hundred pies. They'd do strawberry, lemon and lime.

"There's really not much to a chiffon pie," Lois had assured Hannah when they'd agreed to everything. Breakfast was over and the day had been leaning toward lunch time. Hannah knew the ranch hands were going to need to work late to make up for the time they were taking, and she had appreciated it.

"There's enough to them to charge twenty-five dollars per pie," Randy had said firmly at the time. "Don't take a penny less."

"But we only charge ten dollars ordinarily," Lois protested.

At the time, Hannah couldn't help but notice the slight flush on Lois's face as she talked with the wrangler.

"Most folks will want to give a little extra to the cause," Randy had persisted. "We're just helping them with that. Besides, those pies are worth more than ten dollars."

Lois beamed. "Really?"

It must be the praise of her pies that had Lois looking ten years younger, Hannah had thought. After sitting with Lois in the kitchen for a half hour now, though, Hannah thought it was the goodness of the woman's heart that had animated her face.

Lois pulled the back of an order slip out of her apron pocket and laid it on the table.

"Randy and the other two ranch hands gave me their order before they left," Lois said. "They each bought four pies at twenty-five dollars apiece."

Lois grinned as she pulled the roll of bills out of her apron pocket. "Randy said my pies would sell for that much easy on the streets of New York. He said people would eat a slice while they drank those fancy coffees."

"Randy seems to know a lot about pies," Hannah said with a smile.

Lois laughed. "He might at that. He's eaten a lot of them. And he reminded me that we do include a tin pie plate," Lois added. "We don't charge for that. It's reusable, too.

"Anyway, the three hundred dollars we got from Randy and his friends will help us order supplies," Lois said.

"That's not going to buy enough supplies to make all those pies," Hannah said.

"I'm sure our boss, Linda, will let us use her supplies," Lois said. "And I have enough in savings to pay for everything if she doesn't."

"The first money from the pies will go to reimbursing whoever buys the supplies," Hannah said.

"We'll talk about that after we sell those pies," Lois said as she stood. "Someone's coming."

It took Hannah another second, but then she heard the sound of an oncoming vehicle, too. While the person driving that vehicle might be going to the hardware store or the church, the odds were good that they would be stopping at the café.

Hannah walked out to the front of the café as Mark walked into the place carrying a furry bundle.

"You have Jeremy's cat," Hannah exclaimed in astonishment. "How'd you manage that? The beast never leaves his side."

Mark didn't appear any more pleased to be carrying the cat than Callie looked to be carried. When they were inside and Mark had closed the door, he released his hold and the cat jumped to the floor.

"I don't think the cat should be here," Hannah said. "In most cafés where I've worked, the health inspectors will grade a place down if they allow pets inside the main area."

"Callie's already been in here," Lois reminded everyone as she walked out from the kitchen. "We disinfect the floors every night anyway."

"I was just hoping to buy a can of tuna," Mark said as he reached for the cat and lifted her up into his arms. "I'll keep her from parading around."

"I'll get a can," Lois said as she started back toward the kitchen.

"Tuna?" Hannah asked, feeling like she was missing some steps in this story. That cat barely tolerated strangers. Hannah wasn't even allowed to hold her without enduring the threat of claws. "How did you end up with Callie?"

"She wanted my sandwich," Mark said as though that explained everything. "Until I pulled off the road on the way back and she saw that I mix pickles and onion with my tuna. Then she didn't want to have anything to do with it. She probably wasn't too impressed with the mayonnaise, either."

"Jeremy has some food for her over at Mrs. Hargrove's," Hannah said. She was beginning to understand. "But you don't have to bribe the cat with tuna. She can't coax Jeremy to accept you."

"I wouldn't count on that," Mark said as Lois returned and gave him a small can that had the lid removed. "This is a cat that knows how to get her way."

With that, Mark turned and took Callie out of the café. Hannah stepped over to the window so she could see Mark sit on the café steps. He set the opened can of tuna on the ground and let Callie down. The cat didn't even bother to turn and give him a thank-you glance. Instead, she went directly to the can and started to eat like she'd missed a week of meals.

Hannah turned and saw that Lois had come to stand beside her.

"That man is trying awful hard to get Jeremy's attention," Hannah said.

Lois smiled. "It's you he's trying to impress."

Hannah shook her head. "How can I encourage any man unless Jeremy accepts him?"

"Maybe Jeremy will follow your lead," Lois said. "He's not a difficult child to please, but he sure doesn't want to go against you."

With that, the waitress walked away from the window and started back to the kitchen. Before she got to that doorway, though, she turned and said, "Just don't let Mark get away if he's the one you want in your heart."

Hannah didn't answer. She didn't dare rely on her heart. Emotions had not served her well in the past. She'd been so young when she loved Mark before.

*Dear Lord*, she prayed. *Give me wisdom in this.*

Then she heard Lois come back from the kitchen with a broom in her hand.

"It's been too long since we swept off the front steps," Lois said as she held out the scruffy-looking thing to Hannah.

"Okay," Hannah said as she grabbed the broom and the excuse Lois gave her before heading for the door.

# *Chapter Twelve*

Mark guarded the cat as she stood in front of him and ate her tuna. If he didn't know she had been abandoned before Jeremy got her, he would worry that she would run away just to spite him. But a stray cat would stay until the tuna was gone.

"I know you didn't figure on a trip to Miles City when you went hunting that sandwich." Mark felt a little sorry for the animal once he thought about her hard life.

Then he heard the café door open behind him and looked up to see Hannah standing there with a tall, wicked-looking broom in her hand. The straws in the broom stuck out in all directions.

"I didn't know you liked cats," Hannah said as she swept the broom across the weathered boards of the porch. Puffs of dust flew up, and she frowned as she looked down at the straw that had fallen from the broom.

Mark decided that, since she was looking down, he could gaze at her all he wanted. The afternoon sun was shining on her hair, and even though it was pulled back into a ponytail, he could see the copper strands shimmer as she turned to talk to him. She was an exciting woman.

"Or maybe I'm wrong," she added.

"Huh?" he said, startled out of his reverie.

"The cat," she reminded him. "You like her?"

"The cat and I are learning to understand each other," Mark said. "I didn't exactly invite her to come along with me. She snuck into my cab. I don't know how she feels about me, though."

"She wouldn't have gone with you if she didn't know Jeremy liked you," Hannah said. "Cats sense those things and wild cats more than most. So she likes you well enough."

Mark thought about that a minute. "You think so? It's not just the tuna?"

Hannah nodded as she leaned the broom in a corner of the railing and sat down on the top step. "That cat was afraid of men for the longest time. She didn't really settle in until she adopted Jeremy. Even then she didn't like strangers, especially men."

"She may like me okay, but can I trust her?" Mark said thoughtfully.

"Trust her for what?" Hannah said with an arch to her voice. "She's a cat."

"I wonder whether or not she'll cause a fuss when she sees Jeremy," Mark clarified. "She can make him think I took her against her will. She can doom me in Jeremy's eyes. He trusts her a lot more than he trusts me."

Mark didn't want Hannah to see how worried he was, but he could hardly hide it.

"I'll vouch for you," Hannah said, sounding impulsive as she leaned down and put her hand on his shoulder.

Mark didn't know if it was the comfort of her gesture or the words she said, but his world tilted on its axis. He'd been lost and now he was found. He had his bearings.

"You're saying you want me to be a father to Jeremy?" he asked just to be sure he wasn't misunderstanding.

Hannah nodded. "I don't promise I won't sometimes feel insecure. Jeremy is all I have. But I want the best for him and I think he'll be fortunate to have you in his life as his father."

Mark wanted to ask if she wanted him in her life, too, but he realized he was a coward. She might say no and that would jeopardize everything. She might even decide then that Jeremy didn't need him, either.

For the first time, Mark felt a kinship with Randy Collins. When so much rested on a yes or a no, it was hard to ask a woman for her answer. Doubt was easier to live with than rejection.

Hannah was studying him intently, her hazel eyes searching for something on his face.

"I would never hurt you," Mark vowed. "You don't need to worry about me trying to take Jeremy away from you."

Hannah nodded slowly.

Mark swallowed and attempted a smile. "I might have to get myself a cape and learn how to fly to compete with his comic book heroes, but I promise to do my best to keep our son happy and safe." He thought a moment. "And healthy. Especially that."

"I know you will," Hannah assured him quietly.

"But I won't ask him to choose between the two of us," Mark said.

They sat together in silence for a bit. The sun was

getting ready to take its long journey into the dark night. There had been no clouds at all today so the rain that everyone had expected had fallen elsewhere. No vehicles went by on the rough road. He could hear the sounds of distant hammering and wondered about the large old house on the outskirts of Dry Creek that was being converted into a bed-and-breakfast.

"This is a good place for Jeremy to grow up," Mark said.

"I don't want him to feel out of place," Hannah said. "Since he wasn't born here or anything."

Mark was surprised. "What do you mean, he wasn't born here? Where was he born?"

Hannah gave a tight smile. "It doesn't matter, but I went to a place for unwed mothers up on the Hi-Line."

"Oh," Mark said. For the first time, he began to picture what Hannah's days had been like when she was pregnant. He'd always assumed she'd been here in Dry Creek where Mrs. Hargrove would look out for her and the community would have pressured Mr. Stelling to help her.

"You were all alone," he said, his voice stark. It wasn't a question; he didn't need an answer. He doubted she had known anyone up there.

"Jeremy was worth it," Hannah said fiercely. "Every minute of it. But sometimes I worry what would happen to him if anything were to happen to me."

Mark's stomach clenched. "Are you sick?"

Hannah shook her head. "But things happen all the time. My dad just had that accident. It could have been me and it could have been worse."

"So," Mark said. He was trying to figure this out.

"I'm the one who will be there for disaster management?"

Hannah nodded. "Something like that."

"But I want to be there for the day-to-day things, too," Mark protested. He felt a little desperate. "For the boring Sunday afternoons, for the picnics when the mosquitoes torment everyone, even for the bad report cards and the visits to the principal's office."

"Well, maybe I could—" Hannah was clearly prepared to negotiate with him, and Mark's heart sank. She wasn't going to stay here. She'd accept his help in getting Jeremy well, but she wasn't planning on having a future with him. He'd be relegated to a few weekends of visitation in the summer and monthly duty letters. Mark let his options reach out in front of him.

Then he decided it would not do. He would save Jeremy in such a blaze of glory that Hannah would be forced to think twice about living her life without him. Women always liked a winner. He'd learned that in high school.

"Is Jeremy at Mrs. Hargrove's place?" he asked.

Hannah nodded. "She called a little bit ago to let me know he was up from his nap. She knows I worry."

"I'll go talk to him," Mark said as he stood and picked up the cat. Fortunately, the feline was finished eating and ready to leave.

"I'll pick up the empty tin in a few minutes," Mark said as he took off walking across the road. He could see Mrs. Hargrove's garage from where he stood across from the café. He'd reach it in no time.

Jeremy opened the door a crack when Mark knocked. He peered out at Mark's kneecaps.

"Mrs. Hargrove said I could answer the door since

it was you," the boy announced, obviously proud of his responsibility. "But not any other time."

"That's wise of Mrs. Hargrove," Mark said. "There could be someone frightening at the door."

"I'm not afraid of anyone," Jeremy said as he held up the hand that had been behind the opened door. He was clutching a comic book. "I've got my friends to protect me."

"Your comic book heroes?" Mark asked in astonishment as the cat slid away from him and jumped to the floor. "But they're not real."

Mark stepped inside the house. Jeremy was staring at him with a stubborn look in his eyes.

"They rescue people from bad guys," the boy said.

Mark closed the door behind himself. He knew he had to tread carefully. "Have they ever rescued anyone who you know?" Jeremy started to speak and Mark cut him off. "Not someone in the comic books. Someone you've met? Someone your mother has met? Someone in your day care?"

Jeremy looked down at the floral rug in Mrs. Hargrove's entryway and shook his head. The cat curled around the boy's legs in what seemed to Mark to be sympathy. Taking his cue from the animal, Mark squatted down until he was at Jeremy's level and spoke softly.

"It's fun to believe in superheroes," he said to the boy. "I imagine it makes you feel safe, too."

Jeremy nodded. "Sometimes I get scared."

Mark put his arm around the boy. "And what do you do then?"

"I don't want to worry my mommy," he said.

"Ah," Mark said as he pulled the boy closer. "But

your mommy wants to keep you safe. So does Callie. And, I do, too. That's what a father does."

Jeremy pulled back and Mark's heart sank until he saw the boy was only trying to get a better look at his face. Jeremy furrowed his brow and asked, "How can you be my father? I've never had a father before."

Mark nodded solemnly. "I can see why it would be confusing, all right. But I was your father all those years when I was asleep in the coma." He saw Jeremy was following his words. "I would have wanted to keep you safe if I'd been awake."

Jeremy thought for a moment and then nodded. "Kind of like the time when some big boys came by and teased me at the grocery store. Callie was in the car so she couldn't get out, but she would have." Jeremy leaned closer. "I think the big boys thought she might be able to get out anyway and they ran away."

Mark pursed his lips a moment. "Something like that, I guess. A father's a little bit like Callie. She guards you all the time when she can. A father does, too."

Jeremy nodded. "Will you sleep on the bottom of my bed at night, too?"

"I'm kind of big for that," Mark said with a grin. "So I'll leave that space for Callie. But I'll come and say good-night whenever I can."

"Can I have a pony?" Jeremy asked.

Mark grinned. "Maybe later. When you can take care of one. If your mom agrees."

Jeremy was silent for a minute.

"Okay," he finally said. "You can be my father if you want to be."

"I very much want to be your father," Mark answered as he bent and kissed the top of his son's head.

Mark turned so the boy would not see the tears in his eyes. He didn't want to alarm Jeremy, especially not when he'd finally been accepted as his father. Before he'd been determined to find the money for Jeremy's treatment, but now he felt his heart would break if he couldn't. Mark had never before realized the sweet burden of having a child. He now knew what Hannah had been feeling for these past few years.

The afternoon had grown long before Hannah went to Mrs. Hargrove's to pick up Jeremy. No sooner had the older woman opened the door than she started listing all of the people who were going to come to the café in the morning to help bake the chiffon pie crusts for the sale.

"Who knew we had so many cooks?" Mrs. Hargrove exclaimed in delight. "Even that new woman, the one opening the bed-and-breakfast, offered to come and bring some kind of gadget she has to crush graham crackers for the crust."

"She is?" Hannah asked in astonishment. She wouldn't believe a total stranger would come to help.

"She's inherited a huge old house north of town a mile or so," Mrs. Hargrove said. "Used to belong to an old gold miner by the name of Keifer, so her name might be that, too, since she's got it now. She's going to make her bed-and-breakfast into a destination place with gourmet dinners and old-fashioned charm. Even weddings. I think she's planning to open around Christmastime."

"Then she has enough work of her own." Hannah couldn't stop herself from protesting. "Why would she stop that and help me?"

Mrs. Hargrove smiled. "I've been telling you, most

people around here are good of heart. They don't need to know you to care about you and Jeremy."

Hannah wasn't so sure about that, but she didn't know what she could say in the face of the older woman's beaming enthusiasm.

"My daughter, Doris June, is coming to help, of course," Mrs. Hargrove continued. "And the women folk at the Elkton ranch. Mark's sister, Allie, will be here, and Linda Enger isn't just letting us use her café kitchen—she's going to round up some high school kids to help, too."

Hannah was overwhelmed. "I don't know what to say."

"They won't expect you to say anything," Mrs. Hargrove told her. "We all pull together around here."

"But I can't repay them," Hannah said. She didn't even know how long she would be living in the area.

Mrs. Hargrove waved away the repayment concerns as she called for Jeremy to come, but Hannah couldn't let it go, not even after she had Jeremy and his cat settled in her car and they were on the road home.

"Do you like it here?" she asked her son. "In Dry Creek?"

He nodded with some enthusiasm.

"Well," she said as she started to think. She and Jeremy had moved every six to nine months for the whole time she'd had him with her. She hadn't realized until now that it was the same pattern of moving that she'd had as a foster child before being adopted by the Stellings. She'd always told herself it was good to get a new start every few months. But, she thought now, maybe that had just been her way of making herself feel in control of the chaos in her life. For the first time, she really had a choice.

"It gets cold in the winter here," she said. "And there's lots of snow."

Jeremy shrugged. "I like to make snowballs."

Hannah nodded to herself. She could stay in Dry Creek. She'd prefer not to live with her father, but he might be willing to continue renting her that small house. Mark seemed keen to help her fix it up.

She stopped herself. That was another thing to consider.

"We'd be closer to—" what did she call him? she asked herself, and went for the easy answer "—Mark. You know, the man who painted part of our new house?"

"I know him," Jeremy said. "He's my father."

Hannah blinked. "What did you say?"

"He's my father," Jeremy repeated patiently. "He couldn't protect me from scary things because he was asleep for such a long time. But he's awake now. He's going to tuck me into bed sometimes, but he won't sleep on the bottom of my bed on account of he's too big. And someday, maybe I can have a pony."

"Oh," Hannah said. "Well, it sounds like you two have it all worked out."

Jeremy nodded. "He lives in Dry Creek, too."

And that, Hannah thought, might be what mattered most to her son.

They spent the rest of the drive home in silence. She was still cooking their meals in her father's house, so she carried Jeremy there after she parked her car. He fell asleep easily and often these days and she figured he'd keep doing that until the doctors figured out how to address his leukemia.

After laying him on her old bed, she went into the kitchen and started to fix a traditional meatloaf like her mother used to make. With a few baked potatoes and some canned green beans, they would have a nice, hearty supper.

While the oven cooked everything, she sat down at the table with a piece of paper and made a pro and con list for whether or not she and Jeremy should stay in Dry Creek. By the time she heard her father climbing the steps, she had fifteen reasons to stay and none to leave.

"Something smells good," her father said as he stepped into the living room. She could see him from the kitchen and noticed he was looking better than he had earlier. She'd have to make it sixteen reasons to stay. Having her and Jeremy around made him happier.

"Mom's meatloaf," she said.

"I thought so," he answered with satisfaction in his voice.

"You haven't let me know what I owe you for rent on that small house," Hannah said.

"What kind of father would I be if I charged you rent on that place?" he answered.

She didn't even know how to answer that one so she went for the other question that was bothering her. "You never have said what you have against the Nelson family, but I think I should know. Mark has decided to be Jeremy's father and I—well, I should know what the problem is."

Her father walked over and sat down at the table with her. "It's not a pretty story," he said.

"Okay," she nodded.

"Old man Nelson was a real ladies' man," her father said. "I hate to say he was my friend, but he was. Even after he was married, he'd get to drinking and would chase women at the bars over in Miles City. Wouldn't even know who they were when he woke up with them the next morning. I know because I'm the one he'd call to go get him. Half the time he didn't even remember what bar he parked his truck at."

The sour face her dad wore told Hannah that wasn't all of it.

"And?" she prodded.

"One day when I came home from Miles City, I found him here. In my own house." Her father was still burning with indignation. "Your mother was in the bedroom crying. He'd been here. She always said nothing happened. That he'd just stopped for coffee and—well, I didn't ask too much more. I knew they'd done more than talk because she had lipstick on and it was smeared. Besides, they both looked guilty as sin."

Hannah was aghast. "You just left it that way?"

"Your mother and I were going through a hard patch," he said. "We couldn't have children and she wanted one desperately. She wanted to adopt and I refused. I think maybe she'd been planning to get herself pregnant but then backed down. After that she made me start the adoption process."

"So it was all her idea?" she asked.

Her father didn't respond, but she knew the answer. It wasn't grief that had eaten him alive after her mother's death, it was vengeance. He'd been wronged by his wife and his best friend.

"I'm so sorry," she finally muttered.

"Was my fault for trusting them," her father said as though that settled things. Then he stood up and started walking out of the kitchen. "I should change my shirt before I eat."

Hannah sat at the table, letting the smell of the cooking food sweep over her. She supposed most teenagers would have assumed their parent's foul mood was because of them, but she'd been convinced her father didn't want her around. And while that may have been part of it, he was raw from the betrayal of his friend and his wife. He would have needed to pick his way through that before he could have shown any affection for her.

She didn't want to make his mistakes. He stewed in his distrust until he couldn't go to church, couldn't speak to his daughter and couldn't even take care of his ranch and house.

*Father*, she prayed as she sat there. *Show me how to help my dad. Show me how to trust people myself. I don't want to be the way my dad is.*

She remembered the verse she'd learned in Mrs. Hargrove's classroom about the sins of the father being visited on the children. In this case, she was the one making this true.

*Please, Father*, she added. *Lift the burden of resentment in this household. Show me a way to trust people.*

## Chapter Thirteen

Mark had been so full of joy over his pitiful breakfast the next morning that his father kept frowning at him. Allie wasn't there to fix their eggs this morning so Mark was scraping some scrambled eggs into a bowl that was sitting in the middle of the table. He wore a dish towel tied around his waist for an apron. Four slices of nearly burnt toast sat on a plate with a jar of honey close by. Mark had set a whole red apple on the table at the last minute in an effort to balance out the meal before pulling out his chair and sitting down.

"You haven't found one of my old whiskey bottles, have you?" his father asked, looking skeptical as he walked over to the table.

"Allie got rid of those years ago," Mark replied cheerfully.

"Then what's wrong?" his father mumbled as he sat down in his usual place. "Besides the toast, of course. It's so burnt I doubt even the chickens would eat it. It should be buried instead of served up with coffee." His father looked around. "There's no coffee."

"I know," Mark said. "We're out."

At that announcement, his father looked at him in astonishment. "You're not going back into that coma, are you? You never forget to get coffee."

"Nothing's wrong," Mark assured him breezily. "I'm just excited because I'm a father."

"Well, I know that," his father said grumpily. "The whole county knows that by now. It's been four years."

"No," Mark said. "I mean, I'm going to be a father. Jeremy approves. I'll take him fishing. Get him a pony someday when he's older. And, until then, maybe let him ride a horse sometimes." Mark stopped and looked at his father. "Whatever happened to that child's saddle we have?"

"It's up in the hayloft just waiting for the boy," his father said, sounding as excited now as Mark was. "Does that mean he's going to come visit us some more?"

"I believe so," Mark said. "Of course, I haven't talked to Hannah yet."

"Oh," his father said and the light left his eyes. "Don't you think you should clear it with her before you make any plans? The mother rules in cases like this."

"She already implied he could come someday," Mark said. "But I'll talk to her today and make sure."

"You going in to help make them pies?" his father asked as he gingerly picked up a slice of the cold, dark toast.

Mark nodded. "I figure I can do whatever needs to be done to help."

"Maybe you could bring us out an apple pie for tomorrow's breakfast," his father suggested hopefully.

"The pies are all chiffon," Mark said.

"Oh," his father said stoically as he bit into the piece

of toast. "I heard someplace that burnt bread is good for the stomach. Like a tonic."

"I've never heard that," Mark said. "Don't think it's true, either."

"Just leave me with my illusions, boy," his father said as he took another bite.

Mark laughed. He was a father. Nothing could dim his happiness on this day. Unless, of course, he thought as he came down to earth with a thud—the leukemia. And then there was the fear that Hannah could move away and take Jeremy with her.

Mark reached out and took a piece of that toast. For the first time, he understood fathers who tried to take the custody of their children from their mothers. He wanted to be a big part of Jeremy's life. How could he do that if Hannah moved far away?

The café was packed with volunteers when Hannah got to work. The sun was just starting to come up. The day was dry and warm. She hadn't slept well, partly because Mark had come over last night after dinner to tuck Jeremy in for the night. They'd been at the small house, the one she was starting to think of as hers. Jeremy had been delighted to have his newly minted father there and took a half hour to tell Mark all about his nighttime rituals. Many of them had been invented on the spot, but Mark played along. When he finally had Jeremy exhausted and in bed, Mark stayed to help her with the dishes.

"You shouldn't have to do this after working all day," Mark had declared as he set the clean plates to dry on the old tile cabinet next to the sink. He'd already settled her at one of the kitchen chairs he'd brought over in his pickup and demanded she watch and not lift a finger.

"If you don't work, you don't eat," she'd quoted some long-forgotten homily to him as she leaned her elbows on the table he had also delivered when he came.

Mark made a face at her then and they both laughed.

The lightness of the moment had lingered with Hannah long after Mark had left and she had crawled into bed beside her son. She still had a trace of the happiness in her mind as she stepped into the café a moment ago.

When she looked around at the volunteers, Hannah noticed the pattern of things. Her boss, Linda Enger, was there and had roped off a few tables for customers. The rest of the tables were designated by different colored tablecloths as pie-making stations. A box-like crushing machine rested on one table along with a few dozen boxes of graham crackers. Boxes of fresh strawberries and a mound of lemons took up another.

As Hannah stood there, Lois walked over with a bag of Granny Smith apples balanced on her hip.

"I didn't know there were apple chiffon pies," Hannah said.

Lois smiled. "There aren't. Mrs. Hargrove is going to give me a lesson so I can make regular crust. I want to make an apple pie and the only crusts I can do are the graham cracker kind." Lois paused and got a determined look on her face. "She won't do that until all the chiffon pies are made, though. We have an important mission today."

With that, the woman took a step closer to Hannah and put one arm around her in a hug. "How are you holding up?"

Hannah blinked back a tear. "Staying strong for Jeremy."

"Atta girl," Lois muttered in her ear.

"And praying," Hannah added in a whisper. "With all my heart."

"Me, too," Lois answered softly. "I've never prayed before, but I'm hoping God listens to me now. That boy of yours is special."

Hannah could only nod her head.

Then Lois stepped away and the work began in earnest. Hannah found herself drafted to the eggbeater table. The other one at her table, Randy, the ranch hand, was thoroughly splattered with egg white, beaten and unbeaten, by the time he finished six hours later. Hannah refused to look in the mirror even though someone—she thought it was Lois—had set up a place for everyone to check their faces before they left the café. Instead, she sat at one of the chairs that had been pushed to the side of the room.

Within minutes, the tables were cleared of their various utensils and covered with chiffon pies that were set to cool.

"Two hundred and eleven of them," Lois announced to the still-full room.

The place erupted with cheers and people slapping each other on the back in congratulations.

"I must have cracked a thousand eggs," Mark muttered as he sat down in the chair beside Hannah. He'd been at the table on the other side of the room from her, but he'd come over several times during the day to say a few pleasant words.

"How are you doing?" Mark asked.

"Ready to sit down, that's for sure," Hannah replied.

She was a little distracted because she saw Mark's eyes continually going to her chin. She figured she had some spattered chiffon filling there so she reached up to take a swipe. "Gone?"

Mark shook his head. Then he put his finger a little to the side of her chin and rubbed at something. "There, I got it."

She appreciated his help, but he didn't remove his hand. Instead he cupped her face gently. She felt the heat of his action inside her and it steadied something.

Mark leaned over and whispered in her ear. "I'm here for you."

"I know," Hannah muttered, and she did.

"I'll be by tonight to tuck Jeremy into bed again," he said. "That's if it's all right with you."

She nodded. "He'd like that."

"I'm bringing over a love seat I found in the attic, too," Mark said.

Just then Hannah heard a stir of excitement in the room and looked up. Lois was walking from the kitchen, one hand held high with something covered by a white dish towel.

"Attention, please," Lois said as she walked into the room, pausing near where Hannah and Mark sat.

Lois turned to face the room, her back to Hannah and Mark.

"Everyone needs to know there's a humble man here who gave us the idea of doing this pie sale." Lois paused, her eyes searching the people assembled. "There he is. Mr. Randy Collins. Come up here, Randy."

People clapped as they all turned their heads around, looking for the wrangler. A pink-faced Randy walked over to Lois.

"As a thank-you, I've made you an apple pie," Lois said as she took the dish towel off and revealed a large pie with a golden-brown crust.

Hannah could smell the baked apple scent from where she sat.

"You didn't have to do this," Randy muttered softly as he shuffled his feet. Then he smiled at Lois and said loud enough for everyone to hear, "But I'm sure glad you did and I thank you mightily."

As he took the pie, everyone applauded. People went back to finishing the cleanup for the day, but Hannah and Mark were close enough to be witness to the long looks between Randy and Lois.

"I heard apple is your favorite," Lois finally said.

Randy blushed at that, going from pink to red. "I like all the pies you make."

Hannah was suddenly aware that Mark had taken her hand gently into his and was holding it as they watched their two friends.

Lois and Randy were silent for another minute, just looking at each other. Then she said softly, "Mrs. Hargrove told me that apple pie is the way to your heart, though."

Hannah felt the pressure on her hand as Mark squeezed it. She glanced over. He was as tense as she was.

A slow grin grew on Randy's face. "You don't need a pie to get to my heart. I mean—" he took a deep breath "—would you do me the honor of allowing me to take you to dinner some night?"

The squeeze on Hannah's hand intensified, but she scarcely noticed. She wasn't even sure she breathed as she watched.

Lois nodded, looking Randy in the eyes with a smile of her own. "I've been waiting for you to ask."

With that, the couple joined their hands and walked to the kitchen.

"There're going in there to kiss each other, aren't they?" Hannah turned to Mark in excitement. "Where no one can see them?"

Mark nodded, grinning. "That's my guess."

"I can see why," Hannah said, keeping her voice low. "This place is full of gossips."

Mark's grin faded and he studied her briefly. "Is that what happened with you? Did people say something unkind when you were pregnant?"

His jaw clenched.

Hannah thought a moment. "I didn't give them a chance. I left before anyone knew because I'd seen how they were when I moved here."

His eyes grew puzzled. "Everyone was curious when you came, I'll give you that." He paused. "We hadn't had any adopted kids in our class. We'd had a few foster kids in the school and some of them were wild, but we didn't know much about adoption."

"Everyone was standing and looking at me that first day I came to school." She could still picture it and sometimes did when she had a bad dream.

"We'd just gotten up to say the Pledge of Allegiance," Mark responded in surprise. "We didn't know you were going to come into the room. We all had our mouths ready to start and the door slammed open. We were surprised. That's all."

"Really?" Hannah said, thinking back. Had things been the way she thought at the time?

At that point, the pastor of the community stood and called for quiet.

"Let's join hearts and hands to pray before we leave," he said. The crowd quieted and reached out to their neighbors.

Mark took Hannah's hand and curled it inside his own. She liked the feeling. The pastor was brief and Hannah felt the love in the room as he spoke. Everyone, it seemed, cared about Jeremy.

"We should go say thank you to everyone," Mark suggested after the pastor said his amen.

Mark was right, Hannah thought. People were going to leave to go home soon. She wouldn't have had the courage to go to the door and thank them if Mark hadn't been at her side.

She was glad when she got there, though. Every person had a kind word for her and Jeremy, including a few women who had been her classmates when she had been living here. She had never thought any of them cared about her and would have been nervous even introducing Jeremy to them.

"I have a son about the same age as your Jeremy," one of her classmates said. "When your son feels up to it, let's get together. They can sit and watch some cartoons if Jeremy's not up for more. My son likes the guy who climbs walls like a spider."

Hannah grinned. "Jeremy would be in his element with your son, then. He's a fan of that one, too. And Davy Crockett for some reason. And any hero who has a horse or who flies."

The other woman laughed. "I have a feeling we need to plan for an extended visit."

It didn't take long for everyone to leave the café, but

the outpouring of help changed Hannah's feelings about the town of Dry Creek. She no longer felt like she was on the outside, looking in.

"They care about me," she said softly to Mark. "I never knew."

He smiled and nodded as he tucked her hand into the crook of his elbow.

"Add me to the top of the list of those who care," he said as they walked to the door. Once they were outside, they headed toward her car.

"Remember I'll be by your house after supper to say good night to Jeremy," Mark said. Then he pointed to his pickup. In the bed of the vehicle, she could see a brown leather love seat that looked like it had seen some wear.

"Belonged to my uncle," Mark said in explanation. "I thought you might be able to get some use of it. He's living in Havre these days and said he didn't need anything that's in the attic."

"The same uncle who had the bed?" Hannah asked.

Mark nodded.

"Tell him thank you for me," Hannah said.

She thought about that uncle as she drove Jeremy home. Not only did her son have a father now, he also had a great uncle he'd never met. And two grandfathers he knew instead of just one. And his aunt Allie.

"You know, a lot of people love you," Hannah said as she looked down at Jeremy.

His face was pale and he looked tired. But he gave a big smile at her words.

Moving back to Dry Creek had been the right decision, Hannah told herself. She didn't know what was going to happen with Jeremy this coming week, but she did know they were home.

# Chapter Fourteen

Hannah woke in a panic the next morning, thinking she was late for work. As she caught her breath, though, she realized the sun wasn't even up yet. The window in the small house was dark. Jeremy was snuggled close to her side in the bed, and she rose up on her elbows so she could see the clock on the cardboard box they'd set up on his side of the bed. She had another ten minutes before she needed to get out of this cocoon of blankets.

She lay back down, but she didn't close her eyes. She looked to the other side of the room and saw the love seat Mark had brought over last night. They'd set it in front of the old fireplace. Jeremy was restless and Mark suggested they all sit on the short sofa together to help calm him down. They had already turned the lights off, hoping Jeremy would fall asleep, so they sat down in the dark.

Hannah would never look at another love seat again without remembering the closeness of that night. Mark had his arm around her and Jeremy was sprawled over their laps. In the silence, she felt the strength of his arm against her shoulders and the taut muscles of his leg next to hers. She felt safe.

She looked up at him, seeing nothing but the outline of his face, and knew she was where she belonged. It wasn't just Dry Creek that was home, it was Mark, too.

Now, lying in bed, she whispered to herself what she had known last night. "I love him. Really, really love him."

*God help me*, she thought as she addressed the one who knew her best. *I really do love him. What does that mean?*

Jeremy stirred in his sleep and she gently patted his back. She could afford to wait a few more minutes before getting up, but today was the day of the pie sale and she didn't want to be late.

The lights were shining bright in the café by the time Hannah pulled up in her car. She had taken Jeremy to Mrs. Hargrove's and laid him on the bed the older woman kept for him. As Hannah was driving the short bit to the café, she saw that this was going to be no ordinary day. People—men, women and even some children—were lined up on the porch and down the steps, apparently waiting for the official opening of the café.

"I'm buying a pie," one rancher she recognized yelled to her as she walked toward the café.

"Me, too," a woman from the church said and then added, "In fact, I'm getting two. A strawberry for me and a lemon for my husband."

Another said, "We're all praying for your boy."

Hannah just kept saying thank you and nodding her head as people called out to her. The line parted to let her get to the door and she was inside before the tears started to fall.

Lois met her there with Hannah's work apron in her hand.

"I've got the room divided still," Lois said in a rush. "But I'm guessing half of the people out there will want breakfast, too. I called Linda and she'll be here in a couple of minutes, and Mark already agreed to come in to handle the pie sales until breakfast is over."

Lois finished and took a deep breath. "There's got to be forty people waiting."

They both heard the sound of another vehicle approaching.

"And more coming," Hannah said as she took the apron from her coworker. "We're in for quite a morning."

From then on, things happened fast. The smell of bacon mingled with that of coffee. Linda decided to set up a small buffet line, and she offered scrambled eggs, bacon, pancakes and coffee for a special price of four dollars per person. She kept the eggs and bacon in chaffing dishes on an oblong table she'd moved out from the kitchen. And the grill was going, putting out golden pancakes as fast as people could eat them.

Mark came in shortly after everything started and began collecting the money for the pies. People were eating first and then picking up their pies as they left the café. It took Hannah a bit to notice that Mark was also talking with the men and showing them something at the last pie table. It wasn't until ten o'clock, when dozens of men gathered outside and Mark went out to the porch, that she realized what was happening.

"He's selling those champion rodeo buckles of his," Hannah said, horrified, looking through the window as Mark raised one in his hand. She glanced over and saw Lois nod.

"But those are his prize possessions," Hannah said. "I can't let him do that."

"I hear he's doing an auction," Lois said slowly. "You know how men here like the rodeo. The prices are five hundred per buckle to start and they'll probably go to double that." Lois paused. "You know what that means. He might make more on those than we will on the whole pie sale. Are you sure you want to stop him?"

All the love Hannah had welled up inside her as she rushed to the door. Love for her son and love for Mark. Surely they did not have to compete. There had to be another way, she thought. She stumbled out the door in time to hear Mark shout out that the buckle he was holding high was now going for seven hundred dollars.

"You can't do this." Hannah found herself squeezed between the café wall and Mark's back. She was trying to make herself heard, but the men—in their Stetsons and their baseball caps—were shouting out numbers and comments.

She didn't know how, but Mark seemed to hear her and he turned.

"You can't do this," she repeated now that he could hear. "We'll get the money someway. I can't let you—"

She stopped then because she was going to cry and she didn't want to do that. Not here in front of all those men, some who stood there with their children and wives.

Mark leaned down and kissed her on the cheek, which resulted in more whooping and hollering from the men watching the porch. "He's my son, too. I'm doing this for him."

"But—" she said.

"I can buy any of them back in thirty days," Mark said. "That's the deal up front with all of them, so if we do get a big loan, I can do that."

"But we might not—" Hannah cautioned.

Mark brushed the side of her face with his knuckles. "I know that, too. It's long odds. But my mind's made up."

Hannah had no answer for that so she just nodded. Mark turned to his audience and she slipped back into the café.

After the auction ended, the crowds melted away except for a few people who came in to get the pies they'd purchased earlier. The last tray of pancakes was eaten by eleven o'clock. By then the coffee pot was empty and the café was out of eggs. Lois made a sign that read No Pies Left and taped it to the window. Mark had been outside talking with everyone as they lingered around the porch. A few families had drifted over to the church, where a prayer vigil was being held.

Since there were no customers left in the café, Hannah decided she needed a break, and she went into the kitchen. She sat in a chair before laying her head down on the table. She'd never talked to so many people in one day in her life. Good cheer just seemed to pour out of these people. It wasn't a cloying thing, either, she thought to herself. These people really wanted to help her and Jeremy.

A couple of minutes passed before Lois sat down beside her.

"My feet will never be the same," the waitress said. "I don't know where all of these people came from."

"All the farms and ranches around," Hannah said as she yawned.

Just then the phone rang in the kitchen. A black wall phone, the instrument had been there for over a decade.

Hannah stood up to go answer it.

"Tell them we're out of coffee," Lois muttered. "Linda said we might as well close for the day. Nobody's going to want to eat here with no coffee and no pie. We even sold the couple of pies I made for the café."

Hannah had a small smile on her face as she answered the phone. She never thought she'd see the day when the café ran out of their most popular beverage.

"Hello," Hannah said into the phone. "Dry Creek Café. Can I help you?"

"Is Mark Nelson there?" a man's voice asked. "This is Mr. Gaines calling back."

"Mr. Gaines from the bank?" Hannah asked as her shoulders straightened. She was suddenly very much awake. "I know Mark was waiting for your call. He's probably just outside. I'll go get him. Just hold on a minute."

Hannah set the phone receiver down on the cabinet and mouthed the words "Mr. Gaines" to Lois before she hurried out of the kitchen.

Within seconds, she was standing on the porch looking for the crowd she'd seen earlier. There was no one around except for a few of the cowboys from the Elkton ranch.

"Where's Mark Nelson?" she asked as she ran over to them. "He has a phone call."

She expected them to say Mark was in the church and was almost going to turn in that direction when they answered.

"He told me he was driving up to that rodeo in Havre," one of the men said.

"Told me the same," another said. "Some time ago."

The third man just nodded.

"But he can't be," Hannah said in disbelief. He wouldn't have left to go watch a rodeo with the troubles they were facing.

"Said he had some business there," the original man said. "Said to pray for him since he'd never been so nervous over anything in his life."

A chill went down Hannah's spine. "He wasn't planning to enter that rodeo, was he?"

None of the men offered an answer until one of them tentatively said, "I wouldn't think so. Didn't the doctor say he could die if he tried something like that?"

"I thought maybe he was going to buy a horse or something," another of the men mumbled. "If I thought he was going to ride, I would have hog-tied him and made him stay right here."

Hannah spun around. She didn't have time to waste. She ran up the steps and into the kitchen of the café.

"Mr. Gaines," she said, breathless. "I can't find Mark outside. Someone said they thought he might be heading up to that rodeo in Havre."

"Oh, he wouldn't do that, would he?" Mr. Gaines said, clearly in distress. "I was just calling him back to say that even though the bank turned him down for a loan, I'd be willing to make him a personal loan of five thousand dollars."

"I need to go, Mr. Gaines," Hannah said. "Thank you for calling."

"You going to Havre?" the man asked.

"If my car will make it," Hannah said.

"I'll meet you there," he said. "And don't worry, young lady. We'll stop him from doing anything foolish."

Hannah hung up the phone and turned to Lois. "Did Mark say anything when he got off the phone with Mr. Gaines earlier?"

She needed all the clues she could get.

Lois shook her head. "All he did was to ask if he could make a long-distance phone call. Linda said yes and then he pulled a paper out of his pocket and dialed a number. They talked for fifteen minutes and he seemed pleased when he hung up."

"Pleased?" Hannah questioned.

"Maybe more like excited," Lois admitted. "But he didn't say anything, he just took off. He'd already sold all of the pies by then and he'd finished his auction, so I assumed he was just going home. That was close to an hour ago."

"I think he's on his way to that rodeo in Havre," Hannah said, suddenly very determined to get there as fast as she could. "Do you think it's okay for me to leave? I haven't finished my shift."

"Like I said, Linda was thinking of closing the place for the rest of the day," Lois said. "Just be careful driving. I know you're worried, but don't go too fast."

Hannah nodded and, with a few last words asking Lois to let Mrs. Hargrove know where she was, she left the café in a hurry and got on the road north.

Mark wiped his sweaty palms on his jeans. It was a hot dusty day in Havre at the rodeo arena and he was nervous. If his life ever flashed before his eyes, he was certain that this arena and dozens like it would be the main backdrop.

Today, though, he was here for Jeremy.

"I made my first real ride here when I was fourteen," Mark said, loud enough for the sound to go through to the recording device. He was fortunate to be the same size as Jacob Marsh, one of his wrangler friends, and he was doubly fortunate that the man had agreed to change clothes with him today. The Western shirt he now wore was made of the most expensive cotton he'd ever had on, and the snaps down its front sparkled in the sun like diamonds. In fact, knowing Jacob, there might be diamond chips in them somewhere.

Jacob had bought one of Mark's belt buckles this morning and was lending it to him for the day, as well. The black Stetson, with its braided leather band, was the crowning touch if one didn't count the finely tooled black leather boots on his feet.

"Don't mind the dust," the cameraman said to someone as a chute opened on their left.

Mark turned to look. That Brahma bull making trouble there was one he knew well. The beast turned its head in the chute and pawed at the ground as a man gingerly dropped down on its back.

"That was me when I was sixteen," Mark continued on for the camera. He lowered his voice so the rider wouldn't hear. "Scared me spitless, I'll tell you that much."

"Why'd you do it, then?" the cameraman asked.

"I always had to win," he answered simply. "I thought it made me a better man to be able to do something faster and better than someone else."

It also made him think it caused people to love him, but he wasn't going to say that.

"I know better now," he said instead.

Just then the chute's outer door was opened and the bull charged out into the arena. Mark thought he heard someone calling his name as the rider lifted his arm to balance his wild ride.

"Mark." He heard the voice louder and looked behind him. The crowd was parting for some reason.

"Hannah?" he asked as she came barreling toward him. Her hair had fallen out of her ponytail and spun around her like golden brass. Her eyes were wide. She was breathing deep and her legs were moving fast.

He opened his arms and she ran right into them.

"What's wrong?" he asked, worried by now that something was happening. "Something with Jeremy?"

Hannah shook her head, but seemed unable to speak. She kept taking big gulps of air. If he wasn't holding her steady with his arms, he was afraid she'd pass out. He'd never seen her so distraught.

Since it wasn't their son causing her to be so agitated, he didn't know what it could be. "Something wrong with your father?"

She shook her head.

"It's you," she finally gasped.

"Me?" he asked, dumbfounded.

"Yes, you," she said, her voice louder now that she seemed to have regained her breath. "You can't ride in this rodeo. I don't care what you think, you can't. We just got you back. We can't lose you again."

Mark felt the smile growing as his lips stretched. "So you'd miss me if I was gone?"

"Of course," Hannah retorted, her eyes flashing at him.

Mark tightened his arms until she was comfortably close to his chest. "I'd miss you, too." He leaned closer to whisper in her ear. "I happen to love you, Hannah Stelling."

He felt a little contented sigh, and then Hannah seemed to remember something because she reared back far enough to look him in the eyes. "Well, then, what are you doing here?"

"I'm doing the first part of a media package for the tabloid folks that want my story," Mark said. "Since they already had a stringer up here today for the rodeo, we're getting some footage shot for ads and such."

"You're talking about your coma?" Hannah asked in astonishment.

Mark nodded.

"If they make me out to be an oddity," he said, "I'll just live with it. I have more important things in my life now than my pride."

At that point, the cameraman called out, "Introduce us to the lady. What part does she play in the story?"

"She's the love of my life," Mark answered. It took all his courage to look down at Hannah staring up at him a riot of emotions flooding her face.

"You getting married?" the cameraman called out again. "Viewers want to know."

Mark turned his back to the camera with Hannah still in his arms. Some things were private.

"I plan to ask you, but you don't have to say anything right now," he rushed to assure Hannah. "I know this is a little public and you like your privacy. And you probably don't want to think about anything until Jeremy is settled and—"

Hannah put her fingers to his lips. "Yes."

"Yes?" he asked in surprise.

Hannah nodded, a smile growing on her face. "Yes."

Mark spun them around. "The answer is yes. She's going to marry me."

He hadn't noticed, but by that time a small crowd had gathered. People still knew the name Mark Nelson when they went to a rodeo. And then he saw Mr. Gaines from the bank.

"She's going to marry me," he called out to the banker just in case he hadn't been able to hear in all the noise of the rodeo.

The camera continued to roll and Mark realized he hadn't even been able to tell Hannah that he had a cashier's check in his pocket for twenty thousand dollars. It seemed that the tabloid company not only had money, they knew how to use it and could get it to someone faster than he ever thought possible.

As the rodeo announcer blared out the results of the last ride, Mark signaled the cameraman that he wanted a few minutes alone with Hannah. The man grinned and turned the crowd toward the rodeo winner.

Mark led Hannah behind the bleachers and turned her to face him.

"You really are okay with this?" he asked. "It's not how I intended to propose."

Hannah shrugged. "We'll have a story to tell Jeremy."

"And our other kids," Mark added with a grin. "Although I still intend to take you out for a romantic candlelight dinner. Just as soon as—"

He didn't finish, but then, he didn't need to. They both knew Jeremy's health was the only missing piece in their happiness. Hannah closed her eyes as she leaned against his chest and he put his arms around her.

"We can only trust in God," he said as he held her. He felt her nod and he felt peace.

"Be with us," he prayed. "And our son."

## Chapter Fifteen

Mark took his cashier's check into the doctor's office on Monday morning and, after a quick trip to Mark's bank, they scheduled Jeremy's procedure for two days later. Hannah kept working at the café and Mark took those two days to work on repairing her small house. He wanted Jeremy to come home to a bright, clean place. Randy helped Mark both days and they got almost everything done. The walls inside were now all yellow or white. The linoleum had been replaced. Allie had made white eyelet curtains for the windows. There were some leftover blue tiles from Allie's new kitchen, enough to line the counters in Hannah's kitchen, as well.

Wednesday morning was overcast, and Mark was at Hannah's door by seven o'clock. She had a bag of Jeremy's things packed, and they bundled the still-sleeping boy into the back seat of the car. Hannah sat in the rear to hold him in his car seat.

They didn't talk much as the road sped by. Mark prayed as he drove and he could hear Hannah doing the same thing in the back. They didn't want to disturb Jeremy so they kept their voices low. The boy was increasingly frail and pale. Mark wondered if Jeremy would have the strength for any procedure.

By the time they arrived at the cancer center, their nerves were all stretched thin. The staff there was expecting them, and the three of them were shown to a room where they would wait for the doctor.

"They'll be ready for Jeremy soon," a nurse informed them before she left. Mark could hear the woman's footsteps as she walked down the hall.

Mark looked at Hannah as she cuddled Jeremy to her. The brightness of her hair against their son's face made the boy's skin look even whiter. Mark wished he could press more life into both of them. These two people held his heart and it was breaking.

"Time to go," the nurse came back to the door and announced.

Mark and Hannah both stood up.

"Only one of you can go with Jeremy," the nurse said crisply.

"But—" Both Mark and Hannah protested as one.

"Doctor's orders," the woman said, looking determined.

"Well, I—" Hannah started to say something as she looked at Mark.

He smiled. "No, you should go." He would be fine. She was their son's mother.

"If you're sure," Hannah said.

Mark nodded. "I'll stay here and pray."

"Thank you," Hannah murmured and bent down to look Jeremy in the eyes.

"Do you want your comics?" she asked as she rummaged through the bag she'd brought. She pulled out two of the colorful books and held them out to the boy.

Jeremy looked at them for a bit and then shook his head. "I don't need them anymore."

He held out a small hand to Mark and added, "I have my dad to take care of the bad guys."

Mark bowed his head in humility as he took the small hand. He'd never won any prize that compared with having his son choose him over a comic book. He smiled slightly, knowing his friends would think he'd lost it again.

"I'll be protecting you from here," Mark said to his son. "Your mother's going with you."

"No," Hannah said as she stood up. She looked at Mark. "Go with him. He needs you."

"One of you needs to decide," the nurse said. "The doctor is waiting."

"You go," Hannah repeated.

"Are you sure?" Mark asked.

"Positively," she answered. Then she smiled as he and Jeremy walked out of the room.


Hannah watched the door close, tears by now streaming down her face. This small room was square with flat-back chairs lining the beige walls. There were no pictures, nothing to distract her from the fact that the two people she held most dear had just left, hoping to make Jeremy well.

"Please, God," she said as she sat down in one of the chairs to wait. Her prayers were not complicated these days. God knew what she was coming to Him for. She wanted her son to be well.

Then a smile touched her face. Jeremy had been brave to take his father's hand and leave his comic heroes behind. Mark had told her what those figures meant to her son, and she was proud of the little one for relying on his dad to help him.

She realized once again with a start that she trusted Mark completely. She had no doubt that he would protect Jeremy with every breath in his body. More than that, she trusted him with her heart. He would not leave. He would not betray them. He would keep them always.

Maybe she would not have to worry about ending up like her adoptive father, after all, she thought. Forgiveness, she figured, was the first step to trusting again. And Mark had said something about painting the living room in her father's house when he finished with her house. She hoped her father would look at that and learn to forgive the Nelson family.

Hannah refused to watch the clock. She didn't know how long the procedure was going to take and she didn't want the doctor to rush anything. She was surprised when the door opened until she saw who stepped inside: it was Allie Nelson, Mrs. Hargrove, Randy Collins, her adoptive father and—she had to look twice—Mark's father.

"We came in the Nelsons' old van," Mrs. Hargrove announced as she walked into the room. "We brought a mattress for the back in case Jeremy wants to lie down and rest on the way home."

"That's most considerate," Hannah murmured, overcome with emotion. When she added Mark and Jeremy to the group, this was her family. Right here. She had found her home, all right.

Her father stomped across the room and sat in one of the chairs. Mr. Nelson followed behind him, saying something about the new combines on sale in Miles City. Then he sat down next to her father.

The two men were arguing about the merits of different brands of farm equipment, but she didn't detect any deeper animosity.

Her father must have noticed her looking at him, because he turned to her. "Well, they invited me. Jeremy's my grandson, too, you know. I could hardly refuse."

"I'm glad you didn't," she said, and he seemed to relax.

Allie came over and sat next to her. "Mark told me the two of you are engaged."

The other woman had a grin on her face.

Hannah nodded. "We're not making a public announcement until after—" She didn't finish, but Allie leaned over and gave her a hug.

"I just wanted you to know I'm happy for you both," Allie whispered. "I can't wait."

"Me, neither," Hannah said.

The door opened again and everyone looked up as Mark came in alone.

"He's resting," Mark assured everyone, but his eyes searched for Hannah. "The doctor said he'll be here in a few minutes and give us an update, but everything looks good."

Mark started walking over to where Hannah sat, but before he got that far, the doctor came in and everyone stood up.

"Quite the family here," the doctor said as he looked around.

Hannah held her breath and stepped closer to Mark. He put his arm around her.

"Well, you all want to know about Jeremy," the doctor continued. "As I told his father—" he nodded toward Mark "—the procedure was a success. There's a good chance—ninety-eight percent, I'd say—that Jeremy will be able to keep his leg and won't have impaired function. I believe the leukemia will be in check, too, although we can't be sure of that at this point."

Hannah felt her breath return to normal as Mark rubbed her back and the others started to talk among themselves excitedly.

"We did it," Mark leaned close and whispered.

"We sure did," she said as she turned until they were face-to-face.

Suddenly, all she could see were his eyes gazing at her with his heart full of emotions.

"I love you, Hannah Stelling soon-to-be Nelson," Mark said.

She smiled, and then he kissed her long and full until she couldn't even hear the exclamations from everyone else in the room.

## Epilogue

It was late November when Hannah stood in the small room off the foyer of the church in Dry Creek and asked herself how much happiness a person's heart could hold. Hers was bursting as she waited. The smell of roses permeated the whole church. The door of the side room was open an inch, and she could see into the sanctuary enough to know the stained-glass windows had cast a golden hue over the many neighbors and friends who were seated in the pews.

Finally, the pianist started to play. Hannah stood straighter. One hand was hidden behind a large bouquet of roses and the other was tucked into the folds of the most beautiful wedding dress she'd ever seen. Her adoptive mother had worn this gown at her own wedding years ago. The white silk and ivory lace made Hannah feel like she was a very special princess.

She looked over to where her father stood beside her. "I can't thank you enough for the dress."

He acknowledged her words with a nod and a smile. "It's right that you have it. Your mother would be proud to see you in it. And—" he looked down "—it does my heart good, too. I'm going to do better by you and Jeremy from here on out."

Hannah blinked. She still wasn't used to having a parent who cared about her, but her father seemed determined to prove himself and she was going to let him. She wanted a close family tie with him even when she was married to Mark.

"Is it time now, Mommy?" Jeremy looked up at her and asked eagerly. He was standing in front of her, his arms resting on the handles of his crutches. She was grateful for his medical care. He wasn't going to need a wheelchair, but Jeremy did need to use the crutches for a few more months while his leg finished healing. The leukemia was in remission and the doctor thought it would likely stay that way for years.

Just then the tempo of the music changed and Hannah knew it was time to go into the sanctuary. Mrs. Hargrove, who had remained in the entryway to help them with any last-minute adjustments, opened the door quietly and then stood aside. The older woman planned to slip into the sanctuary when Hannah had reached the front of the church.

"You can go now, sweetheart," Hannah whispered to Jeremy. He was wearing a boy-sized tuxedo and he had the rings pinned to his collar. As he proudly started through the doorway and down the aisle, Hannah could see the white handkerchiefs come out from pockets and purses all over the sanctuary. The whole community had cheered Jeremy on as he fought his way back to full health. Now they let their happiness show. Jeremy's walk today was about more than the wedding; it was a triumphant march for everyone to see.

Hannah let Jeremy get halfway down the aisle before she pressed against her father's arm, letting him know it was time for them to begin their long walk.

She started blinking back tears before she'd taken two steps at her father's side. Mark was waiting for her at the end of the aisle and his eyes were glowing with love as he watched her come toward him. From that point on, she didn't notice anyone else.

The vows went by in a whirlwind. Mrs. Hargrove had pinned the rings on Jeremy's collar so they came off easily into the pastor's hands. Mark cradled Hannah's hand as he slipped the ring onto her finger. She managed to slide his ring on almost as smoothly as he had done with hers.

And then the pastor announced that Mark could kiss his bride.

A smile lit up her new husband's face as Hannah stood there, suddenly aware of the glad whispers from their friends as they rose up from the pews.

"I love you," Mark murmured as he lowered his head to hers.

Hannah meant to say she loved him, too, but his lips found hers before she could form the words and then the joy of the kiss filled her so completely she was beyond speech.

Fortunately, her son was still capable of talking.

"Love, too," Jeremy said as he leaned into Mark and Hannah, leaving his crutches to dangle slightly as he held on to them both.

Hannah felt Mark's lips pull away from hers and

saw him smile as he glanced down. Together they each put an arm down to steady Jeremy as he stood with them. They were a family, Hannah told herself. She had come home.

* * * * *

*If you liked this story,*
*pick up these other heartwarming books*
*from Janet Tronstad:*

Sleigh Bells for Dry Creek
Lilac Wedding in Dry Creek
Wildflower Bride in Dry Creek
Second Chance in Dry Creek
White Christmas in Dry Creek
Alaskan Sweethearts
Easter in Dry Creek

*Available now from Love Inspired!*

*Find more great reads at www.LoveInspired.com*

Dear Reader,

I am delighted you picked up this book to read. I love telling stories set in my small fictitious town of Dry Creek, Montana, and am delighted when readers like you choose to share the adventure with me. Over the years, the themes of my Dry Creek books have varied, but this is the first one that has fatherhood front and center. Being a parent probably changes everyone who takes the role seriously. In *Dry Creek Daddy*, Mark Nelson has the added challenge of having been in a coma for the first few years of his son's life. His young son isn't even sure he wants a father.

I like to hear from my readers and, if you'd like to contact me after reading the book, I would be very pleased. You may email me through my website at www.janettronstad.com.

May you be blessed with all good things.

Sincerely,
*Janet Tronstad*

# COMING NEXT MONTH FROM
## Love Inspired®

### Available September 18, 2018

## THE AMISH CHRISTMAS COWBOY
*Amish Spinster Club* • *by Jo Ann Brown*

Though Texan cowboy Toby Christner was raised Amish, he has no plans to settle down in the new community along Harmony Creek. But when he meets Amish nanny Sarah Kuhns, he can't help but wonder if a Plain life with her is exactly what he needs.

## AN AMISH HOLIDAY WEDDING
*Amish Country Courtships* • Carrie Lighte

To bring in more revenue, Amish baker Faith Yoder needs to hire a delivery person to bring her treats to a nearby Christmas festival—and Hunter Schwartz is perfect for the job. They're both determined not to lose their hearts, but can they keep their relationship strictly professional?

## THE RANCHER'S ANSWERED PRAYER
*Three Brothers Ranch* • by Arlene James

Tina Kemp's stepfather left her his house, but his nephew, Wyatt Smith, inherited the ranch—including the land the house stands upon. Neither is giving an inch. Can these adversaries possibly make a home together... without falling for each other?

## CHRISTMAS WITH THE COWBOY
*Big Heart Ranch* • by Tina Radcliffe

At odds about the business they inherited, widowed single mother Emma Maxwell Norman and her late husband's brother, Zach Norman, must make a decision: sell, or run it together. Working side by side might just bring them the greatest Christmas gift of all—love.

## WYOMING CHRISTMAS QUADRUPLETS
*Wyoming Cowboys* • by Jill Kemerer

Working as a temporary nanny for quadruplet babies, Ainsley Draper can't help but feel drawn to the infants' caring rancher uncle, Marshall Graham. But with her life in one town and his family obligations in another, can they ever find a way to be together?

## THEIR FAMILY LEGACY
*Mississippi Hearts* • by Lorraine Beatty

When Annie Shepherd and her boys inherit her aunt's home, she never expects the man responsible for her family's tragedy to be living across the street. Can she keep punishing Jake Langford for his youthful mistake, or let love and forgiveness lead the way?

---

LICNM0918

# Get 4 FREE REWARDS!

## We'll send you 2 FREE Books plus 2 FREE Mystery Gifts.

**Love Inspired®** books feature contemporary inspirational romances with Christian characters facing the challenges of life and love.

**FREE** Value Over **$20**

---

*Though Texan cowboy Toby Christner was raised Amish, he has no plans to settle down in the new community along Harmony Creek. But when he meets Amish nanny Sarah Kuhns, he can't help but wonder if a Plain life with her is exactly what he needs.*

*Read on for a sneak preview of*
The Amish Christmas Cowboy *by Jo Ann Brown, available in October 2018 from Love Inspired!*

Toby was sure something was bothering Sarah.

He thought through their conversation among her family's Christmas trees. She'd been distressed by how Summerhays and his wife paid too little attention to their *kinder*, but she'd been ready to speak her mind on that subject.

So what was bothering her?

*You.*

The voice in his head startled him. He'd heard it clearly and, for once, it wasn't warning him away from becoming too close to someone. Instead, it was telling him the reason why there might be a wall between him and Sarah.

Maybe it was for the best. Every day he lingered was another drawing him into the community. Each moment he spent with Sarah enticed him to look forward to the next time they could be together. In spite of his determination, his life was being linked to hers and her neighbors.

That would change once his coworker's trailer pulled up to take him back to Texas.

Sarah gestured toward the *kinder*. "They're hungry for love."

"You're worried they're going to be hurt when I go back to Texas."

*"Ja."*

He wanted to ask how she would feel when he left, but he'd hurt his ankle, not his head, so he didn't have an excuse to ask a stupid question.

"The *kinder* will be upset when you go, but won't it be better to give them nice memories of your times together to enjoy when they think about you after you've left?"

Nice memories of times together? Maybe that would be sufficient for the *kinder*, but he doubted it would be enough for him.

*Don't miss*
The Amish Christmas Cowboy *by Jo Ann Brown,*
*available October 2018 wherever*
*Love Inspired*® *books and ebooks are sold.*

www.LoveInspired.com

Looking for inspiration in tales
of hope, faith and heartfelt romance?

Check out **Love Inspired**® and
**Love Inspired**® **Suspense** books!

**New books available every month!**

LIGENRE2018

Two fatal drug overdoses in the past week.

Exhausted from her thirteen-hour shift in the critical care unit, First Lieutenant Vanessa Gomez made her way down the hallway of the Canyon Air Force Base hospital, grappling with the impact of this latest drug-related death.

The corridor lights abruptly went out, enclosing her in complete darkness. She froze, instinctively searching for the nearest exit sign, when strong hands roughly grabbed her from behind, long fingers wrapping themselves around her throat.

The Red Rose Killer?

It had been months since she'd received the red rose indicating she was a target of convicted murderer and prison escapee Boyd Sullivan.

She kicked back at the man's shins, but her soft-soled nursing shoes didn't do much damage. She used her elbows, too, but couldn't make enough impact that way, either. The attacker's fingers moved their position around her neck, as if searching for the proper pressure points.

"Why?" she asked.

"Because you're in my way…" the attacker said, his voice low and dripping with malice.

The pressure against her carotid arteries grew, making her dizzy and weak. Black spots dotted her vision.

She was going to die, and there was nothing she could do to stop it.

Her knees sagged, then she heard a man's voice. "Hey, what's going on?"

Her attacker abruptly let go just as the lights came on. She fell to the floor. The sound of pounding footsteps echoed along the corridor.

"Are you okay?" A man wearing battle-ready camo rushed over, then dropped to his knees beside her. A soft, wet, furry nose pushed against her face and a sandpapery tongue licked her cheek.

"Yes," she managed, hoping he didn't notice how badly her hands were shaking.

"Stay, Tango," the stranger ordered. He ran toward the stairwell at the end of the hall, the one that her attacker must have used to escape.

*Don't miss*
Battle Tested *by Laura Scott,*
*available October 2018 wherever*
*Love Inspired® Suspense books and ebooks are sold.*

www.LoveInspired.com

## Inspirational Romance to Warm Your Heart and Soul

Join our social communities to connect with other readers who share your love!

Sign up for the Love Inspired newsletter at **www.LoveInspired.com** to be the first to find out about upcoming titles, special promotions and exclusive content.

### CONNECT WITH US AT:

Harlequin.com/Community

 Facebook.com/LoveInspiredBooks

 Twitter.com/LoveInspiredBks

LISOCIAL2017